The Nordic Translation Series

Sponsored by the Nordic Council of the governments of Denmark, Finland, Iceland, Norway, and Sweden

THE WOODCARVER AND DEATH

BY HAGAR OLSSON

Träsnidaren och döden

translated from the Swedish by

George C. Schoolfield

MADISON AND MILWAUKEE, 1965
THE UNIVERSITY OF WISCONSIN PRESS

Published by

THE UNIVERSITY OF WISCONSIN PRESS

Madison and Milwaukee

P.O. Box 1379, Madison, Wisconsin 53701

Originally published by

Holger Schildts Förlagsaktiebolag

Helsinki, Finland

Printed in the United States of America by

Kingsport Press, Inc., Kingsport, Tennessee

Library of Congress

Catalog Card Number 65-24187

Author's Note

This novel is a homage to the lost landscape of a childhood and was completed in 1940, after the cession of Carelia as a result of the Finnish Winter War.

HAGAR OLSSON

Spring, 1965

Contents

Introduction

Anyone who wishes to understand the literature of Finland, whether written in Finnish or Swedish (for the nation is officially bilingual), must have command of certain historical facts: as a land between East and West, Finland has been subjected throughout its history to tensions which have left their mark everywhere in its cultural life.

The Finns, members of the Finno-Ugric linguistic family, came to Finland sometime early in the Christian Era; the first Swedish speakers seem to have arrived on the southwestern and southern coasts of Finland during the Viking Age. In the twelfth and thirteenth centuries, "crusades" were sent out from Sweden in an effort to subjugate and Christianize the heathen Finns; and by 1323 Finland had become a definitive part of the Kingdom of Sweden, in which position it remained until the Swedish-Russian War of 1808–9. For the next one hundred and nine years Finland belonged to the Russian Empire, commencing as a semi-independent grand duchy, only to have the rights granted it by Alexander I at the Diet of Borgå (March, 1809) slowly whittled away by his successors on the Russian throne. On December 6, 1917, in the wake of the November (Bolshevik) Revolution, the Finnish diet and senate, re-established after the abdication of Nicholas II the previous March, declared Finland's independence. A civil war ensued, between the "Red Guards" (many of whom were blinded by simple poverty to the fact that they were fighting for a return of Finland to Russia) and the newly organized Finnish national army, under the command of C. G. E. Mannerheim, lately a czarist officer. The "Whites," substantially aided by a German expeditionary force, won the short but bloody war; and after a year of unfortunate reprisals and political confusion the Finnish Republic was declared.

From November, 1939, until March, 1940, the Republic was involved in the "Winter War" with Soviet Russia, as a result of which it was forced to cede most of Carelia to its giant neighbor, as well as a strip of territory in the north. In the so-called "Continuation War" of 1941–44, the army of Finland, now a cobelligerent of Germany, advanced to the old boundary of 1939 and passed it, occupying the territory known as Eastern (Russian) Carelia. The war ended with the Russian offensive of the summer of 1944; by the armistice of Moscow, Soviet Russia was granted not only the territory it had been accorded in 1940 but also the Petsamo region in the extreme north, thus depriving Finland of its access to the Arctic Ocean. Since then, Finland has walked a tightrope between inclination and necessity, its difficulties increased by the problem of the resettlement of the Finnish Carelians inside the nation's new boundaries.

II

During the centuries of Swedish rule in Finland, the Swedish language clearly won ascendancy over Finnish as the instrument of culture and commerce; it was the major language of the towns and was spoken, as well, in the country regions which had received a Swedish population either before or after the establishment of Swedish hegemony. These regions were substantially the same as the ones which contain the Swedish-speaking population of Finland today: the coast of Ostrobothnia, north and south of the town of Vasa (Finnish: Vaasa); the Åland Islands; the academic city and, until 1827, the Finnish capital, Åbo (Turku), with its skerries; and the southern coast from Hangö (Hanko) and Ekenäs (Tammisaari) to Helsingfors (Helsinki), and then east past Borgå (Porvoo) to Lovisa (Loviisa). There also existed colonies of "inland Swedes"; of these, the most important was at Viborg (Viipuri) in Carelia. Isolated Swedish-speaking families were to be found everywhere in the Finnish regions; the large landowners were members, although hardly typical ones, of this group which comprised chiefly professional people, clergymen, and officials.

Not long after Finland had been incorporated into Russia, in 1809, the country's linguistic complexion began to change; nationalism, making its appearance here as it would, for example, in the Austrian Empire, encouraged the educated classes to adopt Finnish as their language. A movement was begun to make Finland monolingual; it is ironic that its leader, Johan Vilhelm Snellman (1806–81), composed the majority of his works in Swedish. Some of Snellman's contemporaries, such as Finland's national poet, Johan Ludvig Runeberg (1804–77) and the esthetician, Carl Gustav Estlander (1834–1910), felt that Snellman's demand for "one language, one people" was a kind of tilting at windmills; they argued that all Finns *were* Finns, regardless of what language they spoke. Nevertheless, the zeal of Snellman and his followers compelled some Finland-Swedes (for this is what they now began to call themselves, instead of "Finns" or "Finlanders," the latter a word which meant an inhabitant of Finland, no matter what his language was) to take up a position as extreme as Snellman's; the leader of these believers in a separate Swedish nationality in Finland was the philologist Axel Olof Freudenthal (1836–1911).

The teachings of Freudenthal acquired a special appeal for the Finland-Swede of the early twentieth century, who saw how the "true Finnish" element in Finland's national life was increasing its power and importance by leaps and bounds. Feeling steadily more homeless in his own homeland, the Finland-Swede retreated into the protective shell of "Freudenthalism," of what we might call a minority mentality. The establishment of the Republic did not bring with it an alleviation of the minority's fears; indeed, the Finland-Swedish position became even more precarious because of the understandable desire of a nation, suddenly independent after centuries of foreign rule, to become itself, like no other land on earth. The wars of 1939–40 and 1941–44, for all the suffering they caused, did benefit Finland in one way; the Finland-Swedes contributed so generously to the nation's defense that they found themselves more readily tolerated than before. The new tolerance may have also found encouragement in the likelihood of the language problem's resolving itself. The Swedish-speaking population is steadily decreasing, not least because of a smaller birth rate (in proportion to the Finnish-speaking Finns) and migration to Sweden in search of a better life, the very motive which led the ancestors of the Finland-Swedes eastward, ages before. According to the last census, there are 330,530 Swedish speakers in Finland, or 7.4 per cent of the nation's total inhabitants. The figure should be compared with that of 1880, the first year for which we have language statistics (295,000 or 14.3 per cent), of 1910 (339,000 or 11.6 per cent), and of 1950–51 (348,286 or 8.6 per cent).

III

The Swedish literature of Finland has been not merely an interesting provincial phenomenon but a vital factor in the development of Swedish literature as a whole; it provides an example of how a small and isolated linguistic group can produce literary works sometimes more exciting than those emerging from the heartland of the mother tongue, where poets do not feel that the very existence of their instrument, their language, is threatened. No exact comparisons can or should be made; yet the student of Finland's Swedish literature cannot help but recall the renaissance of German-language literature in Bohemia during the nineteenth and early twentieth centuries, first with Adalbert Stifter, then with Rilke, Kafka, and Werfel; or the flowering of Anglo-Irish letters during roughly the same period; or the appearance of one of the greatest of modern Greek lyricists, Konstantinos Kavafis, in the Greek colony at Alexandria.

While still Swedish territory, Finland produced the elegist, Jakob Frese (*c.* 1690–1729), the rococo poet, Gustaf Philip Creutz (1731–85), and the forerunner of Swedish romanticism, Frans Mikael Franzén (1772–1847); all of these poets spent a substantial part of their lives in Sweden proper, the first and last of them having fled there from the Russians. In the nineteenth century, under Russian rule, the Finland-Swedish author stuck by his guns as best he could; the first part of the century was dominated by the giant figure of Runeberg, the creator of the narrative poem on the War of 1808–9, *Fänrik Ståls Sägner* (*The Tales of Ensign Stål*, 1848–60), the author of epyllions on various aspects of Finnish, Finland-Swedish, and even Russian life, and a major lyricist. Runeberg overshadowed his contemporaries, but not completely: for Zachris Topelius (1818–98), who wrote a long series of connected novellas about Finland's history, *Fältskärns berättelser* (*The Stories of the Field-Surgeon*, 1851–66), became a story-teller for the whole of Scandinavia; and the lyric poet, Josef Julius Wecksell (1838–1907), whose career ended in madness at the age of twenty-two, achieved a kind of international currency by the settings Sibelius made for some of his poems.

The ruling figure of the century's second half is Karl August Tavaststjerna (1860–98), the creator of the Swedish novel in Finland; Finnish literature had already received its classical prose work with the novel of Aleksis Kivi, *Seitsemän veljestä* (*The Seven Brothers*, 1870). Tavaststjerna was keenly aware of the growing isolation of the Swedish speaker in Finland, a theme continued by his successors, the novelist Mikael Lybeck (1864–1925) and the lyric poet Arvid Mörne (1876–1946); indeed, a whole literary group, the "flaneurs" of Helsingfors, made the despair of the Finland-Swede its main theme. No one who has read the masterly novellas of Runar Schildt (1888–1925) will forget the desire to die, the *cupido dissolutionis*, which permeates them: two of the "flaneurs," including Schildt himself, died by their own hand, another migrated to Sweden, and another fell into silence after having produced three small books.

In 1913, Holger Schildt, a cousin of the novella-writer, founded a publishing house, an act of faith in Finland-Swedish letters which was richly rewarded; "Schildt's" was responsible for the issuance of many of the principal works in the great age about to dawn. Suddenly, the little literature became a leading force in Scandinavia, with the appearance on the scene of the "modernists"—poets who had imbibed deeply of German expressionism, Russian futurism, and Dadaism, poets who threw off the conservative strictures of rhyme schemes and rhythmic patterns and traditional themes, poets who were determined to win an international audience. The pioneer and brightest star among the modernists was Edith Södergran (1892–1923), born and brought up in St. Petersburg, a patient in Swiss and Finnish sanatoriums, and finally a resident, with only her mother as her companion, in Raivola, a village on the Carelian Isthmus. It is doubtful that Edith Södergran's poetry (which appeared in several hotly attacked volumes from 1916 until 1920, to be followed by a posthumous collection in 1925) could have made its deep imprint upon Finnish and Scandinavian literary life if it had not been for the encouragement and aid vouchsafed her by Hagar Olsson, the young literary critic of the Helsingfors newspaper, *Dagens Press*, and Edith Södergran's closest—almost her only—friend during the last years of the poetess' life.

The example of Edith Södergran encouraged both older and younger poets to try their wings in modernism's new air. Gunnar Björling (1887–1960), a lyricist who would become known for his radical rejection of normal syntax and grammar, made his belated debut in 1922, from then on pouring out a flood of poetry and aphorisms (the latter a favorite form of the modernists). Elmer Diktonius (1896–1961), a violinist destined to make one of his many contributions to Finland-Swedish literature as a music critic of Shavian stature, upset conservative poetry-lovers by means of such poems as his "Jaguar" in *Min dikt* (*My Poem*, 1921); as a member of the political left, and an author quite capable of writing in Finnish, he remained a suspect figure in the eyes of many, despite the authenticity of the genius—and the patriotism—he demonstrated in his later works. Ragnar Robert Eklund (1895–1946) was a poet and aphorist whose affection for his home province of Ostrobothnia, coupled with a patent contempt for all literary and political programs, quickly cut him off from his colleagues: while he contributed to the first of the modernists' little magazines, the bilingual *Ultra* (1922), he refused to take part in the second, *Quosego* (1928–29). In his extreme sensibility and concern with style, as well as in his isolation, Eklund was not without points of resemblance to Kerstin

Söderholm (1897–1943), whose poetry is less interesting than her diary, *Endast med mig själv* (*Only with Myself*), published four years after her suicide. One of the lyric poets of modernism's golden age survives today, Rabbe Enckell (b. 1903), who began as the most idyllic of the modernists, went through a darker phase in the 1930's and early 1940's, and then, after the war, returned to a serenity which on the surface resembles that of his beginnings.

Enckell's example proves that Finland-Swedish literature did not end with the great decade of the 1920's; most of the modernists went on to long and distinguished careers. Contemporary with them there existed, of course, a more conservative strain in Finland-Swedish literature; its best-known younger representative was Jarl Hemmer (1893–1944), a lyric poet whose most widely read work, however, is a religious novel about the concentration camps maintained by the victorious "Whites," *En man och hans samvete* (*A Man and His Conscience*, 1931). The chief literary debut in the 1930's was that of Tito Colliander (b. 1904), a novelist whose background is like Södergran's and whose works continue Hemmer's pondering of good and evil; yet an Eastern element is added—Colliander embraced the Orthodox faith with an enthusiasm evident in all of his best works, for example, *Korståget* (*The Crusade*, 1937), about a pilgrimage to a monastery in Estonia, and *Förbarma dig* (*Have Mercy*, 1939), which deals with a Russian refugee among the Finland-Swedes of Helsingfors. In earlier books, where his Russian emigrants were to be found in Carelia, Colliander had been carried along by a new literary wave with political overtones, the "Carelian exoticism" or "Carelian romanticism" of the 1930's, which combined, for Finland-Swedish authors, some varied charms. It offered the attraction of the Orthodox faith, whose Finnish communicants resided almost entirely in Carelia—a faith apparently more forgiving and certainly more exotic than Lutheranism. (Here it should be remembered that the stock of the religious novel was rising in Europe, thanks to François Mauriac and Graham Greene.) Carelia was a part of Finland where the ancient Russian threat had created a more tolerant and, in the case of Viborg, a more cosmopolitan atmosphere than that to be found farther west. Finally, Carelia was traditionally held to be the homeland of the *Kalevala*, the Finnish national epic, and was the object, in the minds of certain hotspurs in the young nation, of expansionist dreams: Eastern Carelia had already been briefly invaded by a Finnish *Freikorps* in 1919.

In an essay from February, 1941, published not long after Finnish Carelia had been lost in the Winter War, Hagar Olsson called the province "the holy place of Finnish culture," and by doing so summed up the attitude of many authors in the preceding decade, the writers who made more or less pious pilgrimages to the grave of Edith Södergran at Raivola and to the great Orthodox cloister church at Valamo in Lake Ladoga, or to the lesser-known establishment at Konevits, pilgrimages which were turned into books: Olof Enckell's *Ett klosteräventyr* (*A Cloister Adventure*, 1930), *Vårt hjärta* (*Our Heart*, 1933), and *Guldkedjan* (*The Golden Chain*, 1934); Göran Stenius' *Det okända helgonets kloster* (*The Cloister of the Unknown Saint*, 1934); and, of course, Hagar Olsson's *Träsnidaren och döden* (*The Woodcarver and Death*, 1940).

Even after the final amputation of Carelia in 1944, Finland-Swedish authors continued to mourn the lost province; one remembers in particular Oscar Parland (b. 1912) and Ralf Parland (b. 1914), both natives of Carelia, as was their short-lived and brilliant elder brother, the modernist Henry Parland (1908–30). Oscar Parland has composed a series of novels about the fate of a well-to-do family on the

Carelian Isthmus before and after the Finnish Civil War, and one of Ralf Parland's best books is *Hem till sitt hav* (*Home to His Sea*, 1957), a eulogy on Carelia with both mythical and historical ingredients. Since 1944, the attention of younger Finland-Swedish writers has turned to a more urgent problem, the predicament of the group to which they belong: this is the burden of the novels of Christer Kihlman, Anders Cleve, and Per-Hakon Påwals—but an account of Finland's Swedish literature since 1940 lies outside the scope of this introduction. It will be sufficient to remember that the princess of the small but fascinating realm is still Hagar Olsson.

IV

Hagar Olsson was born on September 16, 1893; shortly before her birth, her father, a Lutheran clergyman, had been appointed pastor on Föglö in the Åland Islands. It was in this completely Swedish-speaking milieu that she spent her early childhood; she began her schooling in Åbo, where her mother maintained a separate household for the Olsson children during the winter months. When Hagar Olsson was twelve years old, her father was transferred to Räisälä on the Carelian Isthmus between Viborg and Lake Ladoga; thus the family was removed to a predominantly Finnish-speaking area. During the Räisälä years, Hagar Olsson attended the Swedish Girls' School in Viborg, where she quickly became familiar with the atmosphere of the quadrilingual provincial capital and its Finnish, Finland-Swedish, Baltic German, and Russian components. At the same time she embarked on an independent program of reading from sources even more heterogeneous than Viborg's cultural make-up: according to her diary, she ranged from the *Divine Comedy* to Lafcadio Hearn, from Voltaire to the latest Danish novels of Herman Bang.

In 1913 Hagar Olsson took the "student's examination" which qualified her to attend the Imperial Alexander University at Helsingfors; but her father, a man with set ideas about the place of woman in society, insisted that she prepare herself for a "practical career" instead, and had her enrolled in the Advanced Swedish Commercial School in the Finnish capital. Nine months of training there, and a summer spent in a Viborg bank, convinced her that she must rebel against Pastor Olsson. After a bitter struggle, she was permitted to begin at the university, on the understanding that she would be trained as a teacher, a course for which she had little genuine interest but which would allow her to attend some lectures in literary history.

At Christmas, 1916, her first novel, *Lars Thorman och döden* (*Lars Thorman and Death*) was published, the story of a young man who believes he is about to die and who is terrified at the thought. Eventually Lars Thorman realizes that his soul "has become familiar with death"; he explains his coming to terms with death by a restatement of the parable on the grain of wheat in John 12:24, which later will appear undisguised in *The Woodcarver and Death.* Lars says: "I saw the whole field, where a piece of grain means everything if it enters into the earth and dies, but nothing if it remains a single speck of dust, flying whither the wind blows." Earlier, Lars has seen nothing but terror in death; he has received a shock of immeasurable effect upon beholding the corpse of a dead friend, and since then has been pursued by an entity he calls the "corpse-devil." This violent reaction to death's physical fact apparently has its source in an episode which befell Hagar Olsson herself; on February 26, 1916, she wrote in her diary: "Finally, I might as well come out with the thing that is haunting me: I've seen the corpse of Aunt E." At the end of this troubled novel, Lars does not die after all; instead, his beloved

Lisbeth does—becoming his scapegoat, as it were—while he has gained new strength from his meetings with a Northern Pan, a forest god who bears the Old Norse name of Samr.

Lars Thorman and Death was followed by two other youthful works which must have been still more confusing to their first readers, the prose-poems *Själarnas ansikten* (*The Countenances of the Souls*, 1917), in which Hagar Olsson celebrated "the world's fanatics," zealous beings prepared, like the modernists to come, to fight and if necessary to die for apparently quixotic ideals, and *Kvinnan och nåden* (*The Woman and Grace*, 1919). *The Woman and Grace* is based upon the biblical story of the prophet Samuel's birth; the interest of the author is focused, however, on the mother and the mystical experiences she undergoes before parturition, rather than on the baby, who is born just before the novel's end, or on the father, who dies immediately upon Samuel's conception. Scholarship has called attention to the connection between portions of *The Woman and Grace* and the prose-poem, *Jordaltaret* (*The Earth Altar*, 1919) of R. R. Eklund. Brought together by an article on a Van Gogh exhibition which Hagar Olsson had written for a Helsingfors student paper, the two modernists-to-be had become engaged in 1917; during her visits to Raivola, Hagar Olsson read to Edith Södergran from the manuscript of Eklund's book. The engagement, which forms part of the background of a later Hagar Olsson novel, *Chitambo* (1933), was broken off in 1920.

In the autumn of 1918, Hagar Olsson became the literary critic of the Helsingfors newspaper, *Dagens Press* (later renamed *Svenska Pressen*). From this vantage point, she was able to propagate and defend the modernist cause with brilliance and clarity; her arguments for modernism appeared in book form in 1925, as *Ny generation* (*New Generation*). In 1927 she made a creative contribution to the movement with *Hjärtats pantomim* (*The Heart's Pantomime*), a dream play in the style of the later Strindberg, where the heroine, like Sabine in *The Woodcarver and Death*, tries to escape her loneliness by communicating with an image of Buddha. The following year produced *S.O.S.*, a drama about a manufacturer of poison gas who decides to abandon his calling and is subjected to political persecution. And Hagar Olsson attempted the novel again, first with the curiously evanescent *Mr. Jeremias söker en illusion* (*Mr. Jeremiah Seeks an Illusion*, 1926), about a man who, unlike the praiseworthy fanatics of *The Countenances of the Souls*, is unable to interest himself in any cause, until he is killed in a traffic accident and whisked away by a magical airplane into the "great adventure" of death. From the technical standpoint, her next book of prose, *På Kanaan-expressen* (*On the Canaan Express*, 1929), shows a clear advance over *Mr. Jeremiah;* its greater solidity of texture may stem from the fact that it is less tendentious. In it, looking back over the 1920's, Hagar Olsson concludes that the members of the new generation are branded by the "degradation of the chosen ones," for, by their very self-liberation, they have also freed themselves from older and sometimes salubrious norms of personal conduct.

On the Canaan Express suffers from—and is made more interesting by—the opposition of two views in the mind of its creator; she feels that she must side with the "new generation," which mocks the sometimes sentimental liberalism of the past, but at the same time her sympathy plainly lies with some of the book's older characters. Hagar Olsson's next novel, *Det blåser upp till storm* (*A Storm Is Brewing*, 1930), finds her attempting once more to put herself into the shoes of the young. The book is concerned with a love affair between a wealthy boy and a poor girl in a Helsingfors school; the boy rebels against his father, although he loves him deeply, and ends as a suicide; the girl—whose father, long since a jailbird, has had no influence upon her—can embrace the brave new world without reservations. But there is an almost religious consolation to be found in Herbert's death; moving from the social plane (where Herbert, in dying, seems to be caught in the Hegelian "hinges of history") to the mystic, Hagar Olsson has Sara Ellman, her heroine, remark that Herbert was one of those rare beings "capable of death." "Is not he who passes the test of death the stronger, since death at any event is stronger than life?" Death must somehow be given a meaning; suicide, the voluntary anticipation of the inevitable, is made the paradoxical means by which death is incorporated into a significant pattern of living.

The heroine of *Chitambo* (1933) tries to commit suicide at the book's end, but does not succeed. She is another of those figures in Hagar Olsson caught between two standpoints, this time between an acute and adventurous individualism (her father has given her the name Vega, after the vessel in which Adolf Erik Nordenskiöld explored the Northeast Passage) and a desire to become united with and to serve a community (her mother has christened her Maria). The problems of the novel, in many respects Hagar Olsson's best, are manifold: one detects Pastor Olsson behind the tyrannical Carl Johan Dyster, Vega Maria's father; her lover, Tancred, has some features of R. R. Eklund; the isolation of the Finland-Swede, at once contemptuous and envious of the Finns' trust in their special "historical mission," is skirted; and, at the book's end, Vega Maria is almost shattered upon the realization that the new "tellurian revolution" which she has tried to embrace, the collectivist world of the dictators, will bring endless destruction over Europe. She is saved by a *salto mortale:* she will be like Livingstone, who died in the African village of Chitambo, simultaneously a superb individual and a man ready to sacrifice himself for the masses.

As the 1930's wore on, Hagar Olsson saw that her compromise answer would not do; in her play, *Det blåa undret* (*The Blue Marvel,* 1932), she had evidently identified herself with the sister and brother, representing Communism and Fascism respectively, as opposed to the out-of-date liberalism of their father; in her essays, *Arbetare i natten* (*Workers in the Night*, 1935), she reports with a good deal of sympathy on various expressions of totalitarian thought in European letters; but in the Finnish-language play, *Lumisota* (*The Snowball War*, 1939, first produced in 1958), the father of a Fascist extremist is allowed to speak his piece against totalitarianism, at least in the form it had taken in Germany and Italy, and which it was taking in certain Finnish circles.

The Finnish wars of 1939–40 and 1941–44, parts of a greater conflict, broke off the dialogue between individual and mass, a dialogue in which Hagar Olsson gave her support first to one speaker, then the other. Reflecting upon the situation of Finland, which stood in an alliance with Hitler's Germany against Stalin's Russia, the outsider will readily understand why Hagar Olsson despaired of a solution of the dialogue on a political basis. Instead, with *The Woodcarver and Death* (1940), she pacified her political venturesomeness by giving her heart wholly to Finland—a move scarcely surprising at a time when Finland's existence was threatened, and a move predicted at the end of *Chitambo*, where Finland is called both the "new Atlantis" and the "Africa" where Vega Maria, a northern Livingstone, will follow in the great humanitarian's footsteps. Having taken Finland as her community, she advanced on death, that problem which had tormented her so often in the past, and found its solution in Christianity, a Christianity dressed, however, in the vestments of the Orthodox Church.

In his little manual on the Orthodox Church, Timothy Ware remarks: "An Orthodox Christian is vividly conscious of belonging to a community." He also points out that the Eastern Church concentrates its attention upon the Risen Christ, Christ the Victor, while the West is more concerned with Christ's suffering. The characters of Hagar Olsson who come from a Lutheran milieu are given the chance to enter a church which emphasizes the community's rather than the individual's approach to the divine, and in which triumph over death, rather than the death agony, is foremost in the worshipper's mind, as well as in the decorations and liturgy of the church. Hagar Olsson's next work after *The Woodcarver and Death* is a play, *Rövaren och jungfrun* (*The Robber and the Maiden*, 1944), which takes place somewhere in Swedish-speaking Finland during the famine of the 1860's; thus it is apparently removed altogether from the Carelian and Orthodox setting of the novel which preceded it. Yet its hero, Elk-Matts, a peasant forced by injustice to become a highwayman, is saved from execution by a miracle pure and simple—he flies away, it seems, on a chariot like Elijah's, and a girl among the spectators sees "the victor's crown" on his head; his beloved, Sanna, decides to defy her family's wishes and devote herself to the starving children who have streamed down from the north, becoming one with them. The play, then, is not so far removed from *The Woodcarver and Death* as one might at first suppose; and Hagar Olsson's long essay, *Jag lever* (*I Live*, written between 1945 and 1948, and with the dying words of Aleksis Kivi as its title), leads clearly eastward once again, to the Orthodox Church, which, she argues, has preserved the true message of Christianity, whereas the western churches have perverted it, creating a "pseudo-Christian" culture in which the individual's freedom plays all too great a role. Indeed, her last play, *Kärlekens död* (*The Death of Love*, 1952), demonstrates how a group of "western individualists" torment one another in the rooms of a cheap hotel.

In 1949, Hagar Olsson published a tiny book of prose, *Kinesisk utflykt* (*Chinese Excursion*), which defies classification as to its genre: it might be termed a short novel, a fragmentary autobiography, or simply a journey into the past, the past of her childhood and of nineteenth-century liberalism, which she had made so many of her creations condemn, all the while the reader suspected that their creator loved it against her will. The framework of the book is a Chinese legend, but from China the legend quickly returns to the Åland Islands and the Carelian parish of Hagar Olsson's girlhood. Professor Erik Ekelund has summed up the book, and the tension which in one form or another has marked the whole of Hagar Olsson's literary career, with a sentence in his essay, "Resa till det förflutna" ("Journey to the Past"): "The individualistic will, the strong self-assertion, which Hagar Olsson has tried in vain to subdue by her devotion to the idea of collectivism, by the thought of the many members of society who suffer hardship, has thus [in *Chinese Excursion*] given way to retrospective melancholy, estrangement from the world, and a longing for self-annihilation of the same sort as the Christian mystic's absorption in the divine or the destruction of the ego which the Nirvana of Buddhism represents"—a longing for self-annihilation which, as has been noted above, has long been a main theme of Finland-Swedish letters.

Yet the story of Hagar Olsson's literary production does not end with *Chinese Excursion* or *The Death of Love;* in 1953, Olof Enckell issued a collection of Hagar Olsson's newspaper criticism which proved that she had to be acknowledged as one of the great constructive critics in the

Swedish language. In fact, Hagar Olsson's critical voice is not yet still; in 1963, four recent essays—on the nineteenth century novelists Dickens, Harriet Beecher Stowe, Victoria Benedictsson, and George Sand—together with an earlier work, from 1935, on C. J. L. Almqvist, the Swedish Romantic, were published under the significant title, *Möte med kära gestalter* (*Meeting with Dear Figures*). And, two years before, she had given her public a volume of three novellas, *Hemkomst* (*Homecoming*, 1961), the heroines of which are all young girls, of the same age as Sara Ellman when she loved Herbert Wirén, or Vega Maria Dyster when she loved Tancred. Of the three girls, one is desperately afraid of losing her individuality because her father has denied her existence, the second deserts a humdrum way of life (and a humdrum father and fiancé) for a man who she suspects is a god, the third is so much the individual that she tyrannizes her father.

V

The author of *Chitambo* does not tell us what method Vega Maria Dyster uses in her attempted suicide; she assumes that we do not need to know. Likewise, in *The Woodcarver and Death* a great many details remain shadowy—much more important ones than the nature of the instrument with which Vega Maria tries to kill herself. The reader familiar with the Finnish scene may be able to supply several of these pieces of information for himself, but the foreigner will have more difficulty in reading between the lines.

The principal male figure in the book, Abel Myyriäinen, is a native of a Carelian parish lying somewhere to the north of Lake Ladoga; in the novel, he does not return to his birthplace during his wanderings, which are confined to Carelia's southern part, west of the great lake. The Myyriäinen family has left its home in the country (after the father's death?) in order to come to the metropolis, which can only be Helsingfors; there the mother works in a factory, while the son carves and peddles comical wooden figures. He has higher artistic ambitions; the contrast between these aims and the life he leads is one cause of the unrest which makes him set out for the east of Finland. But there are other factors, too: his longing to revisit his home province, the Carelia which was the object of such various Finnish dreams in the 1930's and before; his desire, so typical of Hagar Olsson's characters, to leave isolation for a true community; and, finally, an overwhelming fear of death which stems from an experience he had as a boy, when he and his playmates spied on the autopsy of a suicide, and which has recently been stimulated by the apparent increase of the power of meaningless death in the world around him.

Near the shores of Ladoga, Myyriäinen meets a band of monks: the reader versed in the literature of "Carelian romanticism" might conclude at first sight that they come from Valamo, the rich and famous monastery located on a group of thirty islands in the lake's northern part. However, we are told that they do not belong to "the large and more famous" cloister, but to a smaller one, which people do not visit "for amusement's sake." The cloister possesses a miracle-working Madonna to which Iivana Lampinen, a Carelian peasant who crosses Myyriäinen's path at about the same time as the monks, wishes to bring his dying daughter, Sanni. By means of this information, the cloister can be identified as Konevits, which lies on an island in the western part of Ladoga, not far from Räisälä, Hagar Olsson's girlhood home. The site has been used in Finland-Swedish literature before, in the book *Från Karelen* (*From Carelia*, 1894) by the Viborg architect and author, Jac. Ahrenberg (1847–1914). Ahrenberg tells the story of how the monks of the island give aid to the survivors of a party of horse-traders who have been caught in a storm on the frozen lake; one of the travelers, in gratitude, lights a candle before the image of the "Madonna of Kazan." The Madonna from whom little Sanni expects a wondrous cure, however, is "Our Lady of the Dove" (*Golubitskaya*), an icon-painting sufficiently famous to have received a descriptive paragraph and a reproduction in N. K. Kondakov's *The Russian Icon* (Oxford, 1927, pp. 80–81).

Even before he sails out to Konevits with the monks and Lampinen and Sanni, the woodcarver realizes that he is entering a cultural sphere "which still stood in living contact with impulses from distant and duskily illuminated centuries, when crusaders from Novgorod and holy men from Athos had implanted the light of Christianity in the people's heart, long before the West came to these reaches with fire and sword." Konevits was founded in 1393 by the monk Arseni of Novgorod; like the much older Valamo (established, according to tradition, in 992 by the monks Sergej and Herman from Athos) it served as a center for the dissemination of Orthodox Christianity in Carelia, to which the free state of Novgorod laid claim. Lying on the boundary between the Swedish and Russian spheres, Konevits (again like Valamo) was frequently plundered, by the troops of Gustav Vasa's son, John III, in 1577, and by Charles IX's general, Jakob De la Gardie, early in the seventeenth century—on the same expedition, De la Gardie performed a similar exploit at Valamo. When Carelia became Russian at the end of the Great Northern War (1721), the monastery was reinstituted, and was especially favored by the Empress Elizabeth. Somehow its main treasure, the Golubitskaya, which had been in the church since its founding, was able to survive all the monastery's and Carelia's vicissitudes, at least until the Winter War of

1939–40. The Orthodox icon, by the way, is not completely unfamiliar to Myyriäinen; as a small boy he had made friends with a little old woman who was a devotee of the "old faith," an oddity in the part of Carelia where Myyriäinen was born. Orthodoxy, to which less than 2 per cent of Finland's inhabitants subscribed at the beginning of the twentieth century, had been pressed back into communities in the direct vicinity of the Russian border. The village—"our village"—to which Lampinen leads Myyriäinen after the trip to Konevits, is such a place.

Iivana Lampinen has the characteristics of the typical Carelian of literature and popular legend: the books of Jac. Ahrenberg are full of persons like him—who are frequently horse-traders: note that Carl Johan Dyster in Hagar Olsson's *Chitambo* has "Carelian horse-trader's blood" in his veins. In Finnish literature proper, foreign readers may remember Rokka, the most remarkable of all the heroes in Väinö Linna's epic of the 1941–44 war, *Tuntematon Sotilas* (*Unknown Soldier*, 1954). Lampinen is all that a Carelian is supposed to be: poetically gifted, quick of mind and tongue, apparently easy of access to outsiders; he differs from the "typical" Carelian only in that he is Orthodox, a special trait which in Hagar Olsson's opinion contributes to his inherent humanity and to the sometimes surprising naturalness with which he approaches religious matters (as in the scene where he relieves himself before entering the cloister-church).

The majority of Carelians, of course, are speakers of Finnish, although they differ, in dialect as in character, from Finns farther to the west; but the village to which Lampinen takes Myyriäinen by no means presents a unity of language or culture, any more than Carelia itself did. In "our village" most of the ordinary folk are Finns, the Lampinens and the Mitronens and Matvej Olkkonen; on the other hand, "the unfortunate Schwancken who ran away from his elegant father and his crazy mother" probably has Swedish for his native tongue, as do, we suspect, the "master of Vornikka" and the members of the family at Lintula—Mortimer, Ottilia, and Sabine. The unpleasant old woman Olsbom bears an incontestably Swedish name, but, socially, is at the greatest distance from the ladies and gentlemen of Lintula; we doubt that she has ever seen better days. Her boarder, Assendorff, and Uncle Ungert have plainly come down in the world, at least as far as external station is concerned. Both are from imperial St. Petersburg, where Assendorff had been a trainer at the czar's stables and Ungert an officer in the czar's armies, in which capacity he traveled widely in Asia. Assendorff is perhaps a product of the large German colony in St. Petersburg; Ungert may again be of German extraction or perhaps one of the numerous Finland-Swedes who served in the Russian armies—in *Vår landsman* (*Our Countryman*, 1897) Ahrenberg describes the strangely split life of these Russified Finlanders. We may recall that the young Mannerheim, later marshal of Finland, once served on a secret mission to central Asia as a czarist officer, when we read that Uncle Ungert, "somewhere beyond Mongolia's steppes, in the timeless stillness beside the river Ljao-he," had come to the conclusion that his life was a "pursuit of the wind"—a conclusion evidently not reached by Mannerheim. Of the refugees from the new Russia in the village, only one, Natalia Ivanovna, the teacher of religion, seems to be of true Slavic stock.

The model for "our village" must be sought in Hagar Olsson's Räisälä and Edith Södergran's Raivola, the latter a village that was largely Orthodox. In her introduction to Edith Södergran's collected poems, which appeared the same year as *The Woodcarver and Death*, and in her commentary to her correspondence with the poetess, *Ediths brev* (*Edith's Letters*, 1955), Hagar Olsson has told us about the Raivola she knew. Traveling into the militarized boundary zone in the summer of 1919, she was oppressed by a sense of unreality in the almost empty train; "but how happy I was when I had finally got out into the road, I remember all my summer days in Carelia this way, warm from the sun and happy and full of smiling charm. . . . This was Edith's land." The opening of "The Arrival," as Lampinen leads Myyriäinen down the path to "our village," comes immediately to mind. In Hagar Olsson's description, Raivola is clearly Lampinen's native ground, "a typical border village with a mixed population and a picturesque assortment of more or less decayed but richly ornamented villas embedded in its spreading greenness." Raivola even possessed an original old fellow named Peck, to whom the Södergrans had given shelter; he is a model for Ungert or Assendorff or both.

Hagar Olsson last saw Edith Södergran in August, 1922, somewhat less than a year before the latter's death on Midsummer Day, 1923. "Edith lay on her cot on the veranda when I took leave of her, I was just about to go when she seized by hand and gave me a strange glance I have never been able to forget. Smiling in her intense way, she said: 'You will still find Christ.' " The prediction was a bold one, since Hagar Olsson, during her student days at Helsingfors, had spoken with a good deal of pride about her "old atheist's heart." But even then, as can be deduced from the debut-article, "Some Questions," in the Helsingfors *Studentblad* of March 28, 1916, she had refused to condemn Christianity straight out; the works she published during the heyday of Finland-Swedish modernism betray a strong urge to experimentation with religious problems. An overt concern with the Christian message first becomes apparent, however, in a little passage in the play, *S.O.S.* (1927): the chemist, Patrick, tells what made him change his mind about his calling. Emerging from his laboratory one evening, he sees some children playing on the street. "Then a little hand was stuck into mine. It was so tender and warm, it lay there, suspecting no ill. . . . I felt a faint pressure. My hand trembled. I looked at the child, who laughed up at me . . . and in a second everything stood clarified before me." The prophecy of Isaiah is behind the experience of Patrick, and likewise the rebuke which Jesus offers the disciples when the babes are brought to Him "that He should teach them." By the time *Chitambo* was published in 1933, Hagar Olsson had become still less shy about her Christianity: at the novel's end, Vega Maria hears a voice which cries: "He is risen from the dead!"

Attention has been called to the Orthodox dress given the Christianity of *The Woodcarver and Death;* and there is sufficient evidence in the book to show that the author has penetrated beneath the trappings of the Eastern church —for example, Myyriäinen, pondering the nature of God after his first meeting with the monks, falls readily into the classical apophatic style of Orthodoxy. Yet, in essence, Hagar Olsson's Christianity is not especially Orthodox; it is her own, and is built upon her own experiences. We have noted, in connection with *Lars Thorman,* that the sight of her dead aunt filled Hagar Olsson with an unreasonable and overwhelming fear of death, the same fear which has gripped Myyriäinen ever since he beheld the body of the suicide; yet Myyriäinen's fear is not just a selfish concern with his own individual fate. Sailing to the cloister with the monks and the dying child, Myyriäinen is tormented by image after image of senseless death (including a vision based upon the widely distributed news photograph of dead children in a Shanghai street, taken during the defense of the city against the Japanese in the autumn of 1937); the shadow of even more hideous catastrophes to come is cast by the hermit whom Myyriäinen meets at the end of the same chapter. The hermit has been turned into a human wreck during the first World War; now, in the late 1930's, he hears the angel of death spread out his wings once more. (A related figure has already appeared in *Chitambo.* Before her attempted suicide, Vega Maria meets Death in the garb of an Orthodox monk; he tells her that Europe's seductive leaders—none of the dictators of the 1930's is mentioned by name—are preparing new and terrible sacrifices to him, to Death.) Confronted by the sure knowledge of his own obliteration, confronted by the slaughter of innocents, Myyriäinen's reason—or, we might say, the usefulness of his earthly existence—can be saved only by a miracle.

The miracle has been foreshadowed in *Lars Thorman,* just as the birth of the fear of death was described in that first novel. In the school at which Lars teaches, he becomes acquainted with two sisters, of whom the younger is hunch-backed; the crippled child dies, and her sister tells Lars what has happened. The child had been injured in infancy by an accident which the sister believed was her own fault; the child, however, lived and died in the belief that a nurse had been to blame. "Even in the moment of death," the surviving sister says, "her eyes were fastened on me with an indescribable love." The makings of a miracle, at any rate, are present, in the child's love; accepting it, the sister could have overcome her sense of guilt and Lars his terror of death, but neither of them understands the strength of the gift they have been offered. The acceptance of the gift must wait for a quarter of a century, until the appearance of Sanni, the dying child in *The Woodcarver and Death.*

Some readers, hoping for Sanni's recovery, may be disappointed at the miracle in *The Woodcarver and Death;* they may have expected a miracle like that which had a theatrical revival in such works as *Das Mirakel* (1912) of Karl Vollmoeller and Max Reinhardt, or *Ordet* (*The Word*, 1925) of the Danish dramatist, Kaj Munk, where a dead woman is brought back to life by the faith of a man long deemed insane. Yet these miracles, contrary to natural law, are not what Hagar Olsson intends us to behold, for they concern only the individual case, that of Lazarus awakened, without achieving the larger and truer miracle of making death—and so, life—have a meaning. The kind of miracle Hagar Olsson will place before us is intimated in the closing lines of the first chapter. Myyriäinen dreams of a tramp on the highway, a tramp who is Jesus. The vision, incidentally, forms an interesting pendant to the cruel novella of Runar Schildt, *Prövningens dag* (*The Day of the Test*, 1917), in which the inhabitants of a Nyland village imagine for a while that a drunken cripple is the Christ. The Jesus whom Myyriäinen sees is not the Jesus who works the miracle of raising the dead—a miracle somehow pointless, since the dead must die again, sooner or later. He is an "everyday" Jesus who can show men the meaning of their "everyday" terror of death, and how to overcome it. For His miracle He chooses Sanni as His instrument, the poor illiterate Finnish girl who (paradoxically like the Livingstone of *Chitambo*) dies in the miraculous realization not only that she has been herself, an individual (her last words are her name), but that she has died in the service of others, a service she performed with love. This love, like that of the hunchback in *Lars Thorman,* has been transmitted to Myyriäinen in two ways: by the last glance Sanni gives him, and by the story of her life he has pieced together. Slowly, Myyriäinen realizes that her miracle has saved him—in a way, it is his miracle, not hers—and he endeavors to transmit the miracle to still another being.

Sabine, the third of the major characters in *The Woodcarver and Death* after Myyriäinen and Sanni, is something of a self-portrait of Hagar Olsson, as indeed all her young girls are: Sabine comes from a cultured but unhappy home, she finds refuge in Bach (Elmer Diktonius has dedicated a poem about Bach to Hagar Olsson), she exists within a frozen mask—in 1912, Hagar Olsson wrote in her diary: "I'm always acting when I'm with people." Also, Sabine has undergone the same shattering experience as Lars Thorman, Abel Myyriäinen, and Hagar Olsson herself; she has beheld a dead person, her beloved brother Joachim. Like Vega Maria in *Chitambo*, she makes an attempt at suicide: her flight in the boat is a not altogether wholehearted move in the direction of self-destruction. Finally, she is saved from her terror of death—a terror that would eventually lead her into suicide or spiritual self-mutilation—by Myyriäinen, and, in a subsidiary fashion, by the kindness of the "uncles," Assendorff and Ungert. And she rewards her saviors: the childless old men by her very presence, Myyriäinen by a devotion which seems destined to become a love of the flesh without ceasing to be a love of the spirit. Of course, we are not told what becomes of Sabine and Myyriäinen; the novel ends like a fairy tale, and so its characters may be expected to live happily ever after, in mutual transformation. Sabine has been changed into a living being by Myyriäinen's love, Myyriäinen into a prince, albeit a clumsy one, by Sabine's. Their isolation has ended: Sabine has broken through the barriers surrounding the dying Finland-Swedish estate of Lintula (which Myyriäinen, a Finn, enters in the novel's last paragraph); Myyriäinen has been nicknamed "the ant" by Sabine—and what creature is more a part of a community than the ant? Nevertheless, Sabine is still a princess, although she has joined the outside world, and Myyriäinen a prince, although an ant. Erik Ekelund's words about the split in Hagar Olsson's soul should be remembered.

Not all fairy tales end happily—not Andersen's *Little Mermaid*, which Sabine plans to illustrate for Myyriäinen. There the prince marries a human bride instead of the mermaid, who has undergone such torment for his sake; refusing to save herself at the cost of the prince's life, the mermaid plunges from his bridal ship into the sea, feeling her body dissolve into foam. The pious coda that Andersen added to the story does not erase its tragedy from our minds. Myyriäinen and Sabine belong to different worlds, and it is possible that they will someday be separated. The part of Finland where their transformations took place has vanished. All that is left is the miracle of Sanni; of course, that is enough, if we can understand it or believe in it.

GEORGE C. SCHOOLFIELD

Narberth, Pennsylvania
Spring, 1965

SOME ADDITIONAL READING

The Swedes in Finland

Lindman, Kerstin. "Finland's Swedes: An Introduction and a Bibliography." *Scandinavian Studies,* XXXV (May, 1963), 123–31.

Two useful manuals not included in Miss Lindman's bibliography are:

Dahl, Hjalmar. *Finlands svenskar.* Helsingfors, 1957.
Törnudd, Klaus. *Svenska språkets ställning i Finland.* Stockholm, 1960.

General Works on Finland's Swedish Literature, 1900–1950

Holmqvist, Bengt. *Modern finlandssvensk litteratur.* Stockholm, 1951.
Landquist, John. *Modern svensk litteratur i Finland.* Stockholm, 1929.
Linder, Erik Hjalmar. "Finlands svenska nittonhundratalslitteratur." *Ny illustrerad svensk litteraturhistoria,* V:417–70. Stockholm, 1958.
Schoolfield, George C. "The Postwar Novel of Swedish Finland." *Scandinavian Studies,* XXXIV (May, 1962), 85–110.

Tigerstedt, E. N. *Det religiösa problemet i modern finlandssvensk litteratur*. Svenska litteratursällskapet i Finlands skrifter, Nr. 272. Helsingfors, 1939.

Warburton, Thomas. *Femtio år finlandssvensk litteratur*. Helsingfors, 1951. (The edition printed in Sweden has the title: *Finlandssvensk litteratur 1898–1948*.)

Anthologies of Modern Finland-Swedish Poetry

Carlson, Stig (ed.). *40 år finlandssvensk lyrik*. Stockholm, 1955.

Enckell, Rabbe (ed.). *Modärn finlandssvensk lyrik*. Helsingfors, 1934.

Kihlman, Erik, and Thomas Warburton (eds.). *Ur Finlands svenska lyrik*. 2 vols. Lund, 1949. (A general anthology, of which the first volume, originally published in 1922 under Kihlman's editorship, contains the works of poets from Jakob Frese [*c*. 1690–1729] to Mikael Lybeck [1864–1925]; the second volume, edited by Warburton, extends from Arvid Mörne [1876–1946] to Ralf Parland [b. 1914].)

Wahlund, Per Erik (ed.). *Finlandssvensk lyrik från Edith Södergran till nu*. Stockholm, 1947.

Warburton, Thomas (ed.). *Facklor över jorden: lyrik 1916–1959*. Helsingfors, 1960.

Anthologies of Finland-Swedish Prose

Ekelund, Karin Allardt (ed.). *Folkliv i finlandssvensk diktning*. Helsingfors, 1951.

Enckell, Olof (ed.). *Modern finlandssvensk prosa*. Helsingfors, 1942.

Hagar Olsson

Barck, Per Olov. "Dynamikens apostel," in *Dikt och förkunnelse*, pp. 221–44. Stockholm, 1936.

Donner, Jörn. "Ett stycke historia," introduction to Hagar Olsson, *Tidig dramatik*, pp. 7–24. Helsingfors, 1962.

———. "Ett stycke liv," introduction to Hagar Olsson, *Tidig prosa*, pp. 7–14. Helsingfors, 1963.

Ekelund, Erik. "Resa till det förflutna," in *Synvinklar*, pp. 160–76. Helsingfors, 1956.

Enckell, Olof. *Den unga Hagar Olsson*. Svenska litteratursällskapet i Finlands skrifter, Nr. 324. Helsingfors, 1949.

Lagercrantz, Olof, *et al. Hård höst*. Stockholm, 1943. (Twenty-one essays dedicated to Hagar Olsson, and dealing in part with her work.)

Mjöberg, Jöran. "Den befruktande döden," in *Livets ansikten*, pp. 51–65. Lund, 1956.

Other articles on Hagar Olsson, including those published in periodicals in Finland, can be found by referring to the annual bibliographies published in *Samlaren* (Uppsala). The present novel is the first work of Hagar Olsson to be translated into English. Two of her novels, however, have appeared in German, *Det blåser upp till storm* (*Sturm bricht an*, Munich, 1931), and *Träsnidaren och döden* (*Wie schön ist dein Gesicht*, Vienna and Stuttgart, 1957).

THE WOODCARVER AND DEATH ❧

Now is my soul troubled;

and what shall I say?

John 12:27

One: Dreams

This morning was not like other mornings in Abel Myyriäinen's life. It was not because something out of the ordinary had happened or because some external influence had made him lose his balance. It was simply so—everything was different.

He had awakened with a feeling of intense melancholy. The sensation was so all-embracing and, in some way, unfathomable that it terrified him; but at the same time it gave him pleasure to be so completely absorbed by a feeling. The ground-bass was the same as in all melancholy, whether it appears in a child or in a grown man, in a criminal or a saint: I am alone, utterly alone, beloved of no one. His thoughts circled around this fact with horror-struck delight; he could not understand how, until now, he had managed to exist and had even been able to give his existence a semblance of dogged effort. It was as though an unknown presence had taken possession of him as he slept; in the very moment he awakened he could still feel how mighty tremors slowly fled, and he was left alone and utterly empty. He turned toward the wall and pressed his face into his pillow, hoping somehow, in the warm bedding which had held his unconscious bliss, that he could recover a breath of that intense spirit which had possessed him and without which he knew he could not live.

All he could recapture were some disconnected and evanescent images from the dream he had had before his awakening; a friend whom he once had loved and later despised slipped past in some painful context, and someone who was dead also seemed to have something to do with the matter, but he could no longer tell what it was all about, and besides, it was nothing unusual—for the most part, just the old, familiar story. These confused and painful images contained nothing which could give him a clue, which could enlighten him in any way about what it was he missed so bitterly, which could say why his life suddenly seemed so indifferent and meaningless to him.

He would have preferred to stay in bed. The mere thought of getting up and dressing and taking the work in hand which had lain waiting for him since he left it the day before filled him with a distaste that bordered on loathing. But he could hear his mother rummaging around in the kitchen. There was something curious about her steps and about the noise her hands caused when she was preparing a meal. These sounds were different from all the other sounds in the world. He had heard them through the years, ever since he was a little boy, and there was a melody in them which moved him in a way he could not explain. Perhaps one could have said that everything he had ever dreamed of "becoming" in the world lay hidden in the tune; it had something about it—challenging and cheering at the same time—which he could not resist, even in his darkest moments. He could not let her down, that was what it amounted to.

While he listlessly pulled on his clothes, he happened to think that, for once, it would be good to get away from her, to have a little breathing-space. He had always lived very close to her, in fact there had never been any space between them. Back home in the wheelwright's cottage on the hillside, where his childhood passed in the shelter of friendly meadows and handsome white wagon wheels which even now appeared as symbols of happiness in his mind, space was so tight that the three people who lived there grew accustomed to having even their innermost thoughts become common property. Now father was gone, and the only things remaining from his workshop were the old carpenter's bench and the memory of the enchanted symbol of happiness, but space had grown no greater for the two who were left behind. They had only become all the more dependent on one another, thrown upon one another during the hard years in a strange environment. This little shack on the edge of the big and bustling city had become their silent affinity's refuge; here the air itself was saturated with all the unspoken implications which bound them together. Sometimes it seemed almost oppressively close. Anyway, so much gathered inside a person which one had no right to disclose, hidden things that could not bear revelation. One had to submit to a self-imposed and heavy reticence, in order not to lose the strength which lay in what had been concealed.

His steps hesitating and stumbling, his face dejected, he went in to join his mother. She saw immediately that his eyes had that blank look which frightened her, and which had filled her with dread even when he was a child and had his fits of restlessness; lately it had happened that he was gone for days when the evil thing beset him. "He's got it from his father," she thought, and then all the burdensome memories descended upon her, and she felt that she loved her son more than one human being perhaps had the right to love another.

She rose up heavily from her place and went over to the stove. She stayed there longer than it was necessary for her to get the coffee-pot ready. Quite silently, some tears ran down her withered cheeks. "May God protect him," she mumbled in the dark chimney corner, but her obstinate heart told her that he needed her more than ever just now, when he was in this condition and could not take care of himself.

They drank their morning coffee in silence, and there was nothing unusual about that. But ordinarily the silence around them was full of mutual confidences, of small and mute exchanges. On this morning even the silence was different. They both noticed it, and it bothered them. They knew that they were silent because they did not wish to discuss what they were thinking of. The old woman paid special attention to his hair. He had not combed it today. It was in that tangled and oddly shaggy state which always came over it when he was depressed. The very sight of it pressed a knife into her heart. And there was something touching about it at the same time. He looked like a child when his hair was in that condition. Her own little boy. Why couldn't she press his head against her breast, as she used to do when he was little, and run her hand into his unruly cowlick, and make it terribly tangled, all to her heart's desire; he always used to laugh. . . . He had such a pretty laugh. A weak smile passed over the old woman's lips when she remembered it. It seemed to her he had got his laugh from his mother. But it was a long time since they had laughed together. All of a sudden, she had a sickening feeling that he was about to slip away from her, to a place where she could not follow him. His absent glance made him seem so far away. Would he ever come back?

When she was about ready to leave, she got the courage to say something, something she immediately realized she ought not to have said.

"You shouldn't work so much," she said, and perhaps a little of her old uncomprehending irritability lay in her tone, although she was conscious only of not wanting him to wear himself out the way he had been doing.

He answered nothing at all, but she saw that he seemed to collapse, withdrawing inside his shell. Sheer thoughtlessness had made her tear open old wounds.

She had never been able to reconcile herself to the woodcarving which he occupied himself with now. She held a grudge against it, as against something she could not understand and over which she had no influence. They had clashed about it many times, and if there was any bitterness at all between them, then it arose from this source. When he abandoned his work in the shop, saying that he intended to spend all his time with what had been a hobby of his free hours, she realized that it would end in catastrophe. From the very beginning, she knew that if anything could separate them, then it would be that strange task which seemed never to be finished, and which did not give him a moment of peace or satisfaction. He had never been really happy after that. He lived under constant pressure. Even if he had the chance to sell something, the sale made him no happier. No, she could not reconcile herself to it. There was something unholy about the work, it wasn't like a human being's work at all. People said it was old-fashioned to believe that art was sinful, but she knew better. She could see very well that an evil spirit had got control of her son, since he had started to call himself an artist. He did not serve God with his work, she was sure of that.

She pressed her lips tightly together. She knew that she was right, but she did not want to say anything more. She was sorry that she had said anything at all. Long ago she had decided not to mix into this matter, but to leave it in God's hands instead.

On this morning the old woman went off to her job with

a heavy heart. She fumbled with the latch and noticed that her hand was trembling; then she wondered how it would feel if the house was empty and her boy gone when she came home in the evening.

Myyriäinen stood at the window for a long time, watching her as she went away. He thought of nothing in particular; he merely received within his gaze the image of the tired little old woman who was his mother.

After a while he went into his room. It was his time for work. Mechanically he took out his chisel and his knife, and stood before the carpenter's bench in order to examine the little figure he was working on. He drew back when he caught sight of it. It was like seeing a ghost. The carving, in full figure, was small, no bigger than a doll. It was supposed to represent Myyriäinen himself. He had suddenly got the idea of carving himself in the same humorous manner he used for his other "old men." To tell the truth, he was quite tired of them by this time. His ideas seemed worn out, used up. He had made infinite variations on certain favorite motifs, and he could not look at them any longer without feeling repugnance and shame. Then he got the idea of carving a figure called "Myself." His interest was aroused. For once he worked with genuine enthusiasm. Everything went along splendidly. The sculptural balance and the surfaces' harmony seemed admirable to him. And he had captured the resemblance perfectly. He was terribly amused to see the little fellow take shape, so much like him with his coarse, large-boned build, his stooped posture with its slightly groping air, and his expression, comic in its dejection. In reality it was a pathetic figure; that it had such a comic effect perhaps resulted mainly from its small size. To take one's self so terribly seriously when one is so small: this is funny in itself. He was very satisfied with his little figure. He had a feeling that it would be the best thing he had ever done.

He had even thought this way yesterday evening, when he finished his work for the day.

And now, in the morning, everything was so very different. He stared horrified at the little figure, unable to believe his own eyes. What had happened to it? What diabolical spirit had come and rendered it unrecognizable? It was the same figure, of course it was, the features and the posture and the expression were the same, but where was its harmony, its rhythm, its subtle expressiveness? Where was the artistic meaning of it all? He saw only a primitive imitation of his own contours, undertaken on a lifeless doll. He was filled with horror. It was as though a malicious spirit had conjured forth this dead fetish in order to mock him, showing him the pitiful contents of the being of which he had made a graven image.

Crestfallen, he put down his tools. He looked around the little room where, once upon a time, he had begun his task with such reverence. His glance strayed through the room, as though he sought support somewhere, as though he did not wish to believe that everything he had experienced here had been meaningless. One evening he had read passages from the immortal chronicle of the seven brothers,* and the thought that he himself might walk in the master's steps, contributing with his simple art to the knowledge of this people which did not resemble any other on the face of the earth, seized him with the force of a revelation. He possessed his own province within this people's infinitely vari-

* *Seitsemän veljestä* (*The Seven Brothers*), the great Finnish novel by Aleksis Kivi (1834–72). It is a carving of Kivi's head which Myyriäinen takes with him on his journey to Carelia.—*Translator's note.*

ous character, and he knew this province completely. Suddenly he thought that his vision grew perfectly clear; he saw how it should be, and how the images should be formed to express the innermost being of the people he called his own. Faces, gestures, and situations he had seen in passing came back to him with a new and deepened significance, and he thought that he had grasped the immortal nature of his people. He enclosed himself within his dream-world like a pious hermit, intoxicating himself on visions inspired by his melancholy sense of humor.

How did it happen that now he had grown so poor? Where had his visions gone?

Searching, his eyes glided from one to another of the little wooden carvings standing in mournful rows on the shelves and tables of his den. He grew more and more sick at heart. It seemed as if someone had smuggled his true works away, putting a collection of bungled copies in their place. How was it possible that he had not noticed it before? Of course: he had made forgeries, crude reproductions of the primal images he once had beheld. He felt ashamed and confused, as though he had caught himself cheating. He tried to persuade himself that he had failed because he lacked the skill of a trained craftsman. He had begun so late, he had never received any real schooling, for the most part he made his own way by trial and error. But in his heart of hearts he knew that this was not the whole truth. A voice inside him said: "You know that you have betrayed something holy. Why did you do it?"

In his submission he stood before the ranks of comical figures in order to discover once and for all what was wrong with them. They were old acquaintances, all of them: the philosophical village tailor who resembled a pensive crow, the conceited parish clerk with the adam's apple in his skinny ostrich-neck, Mari the milkmaid, her skirts impudently pinned up, showing her sturdy calves, the old man from the country who scratched his bottom while he gazed astonished at the marvels of the city, the sly old peasants, shrewdly bargaining over some poor nag, one of them praising its virtues in extravagant terms, the other looking suspiciously at its teeth. He was disgusted by the involuntary humor the little figures were made to express. "I wonder what it is people really laugh about," he thought to himself. "If they laugh at the expense of these little beings, then it's wrong. They ought to laugh at their own expense instead—that could be called humor." Of a sudden, he realized with utter clarity that he somehow had lost what was most important, what he had felt most deeply when he had begun. The quality that had enchanted him in these people was not present at all in his copies. He had falsified them, made them less important than they were, so unimportant that anyone who wanted to could laugh at them in a feeling of his own superiority.

"There's nothing immortal about them," he thought to himself. And then he understood that a bungler is not only a bad artist but a bad man.

He returned sorrowfully to the bench where the comical figure of "Myself" stood awaiting its completion. He took the little statue in his hand and looked at it with an expression of sympathy, as though he could not exonerate himself of all responsibility for it, even though he saw how much a failure it was. It was a fine piece of wood, no question about that. Curly-grained, first-class. He always got a sensation of pleasure from the material he worked with. His hand had caressed blocks of wood the way other hands caress living bodies. With his fingertips he perceived the subtlest nuances in the soul of whatever sort of wood it was. A special sense seemed to have been developed within his hand in order that there might be someone in this forest-covered land who understood the nature of the white and mysteriously undulated wood. At its touch he knew gladness even now. And as he stood there with the wooden sculpture in his hand, he imagined that he had stood just the same way, holding a piece of wood, once before, long ago and in another life, when he had been much wiser than he was now, and had known much more about the manner in which wood should be treated in order for it to surrender its secrets. It occurred to him that if he could hold within his hand a single one of those bits of bark at which the little shepherd-boy had whittled so tirelessly, or any of the strangely formed pieces of wood he had found in the forest and concealed in secret places whose location he alone knew, then he perhaps might catch a glimpse of the world of fantasy in which he once had lived. Some clumsy line the boy had cut with his knife, or some whimsical detail nature had created, might perhaps give him an intimation.

"The fir tree told me everything," he thought to himself, and all at once his childhood came so near to him that he could almost seize it. A freshet of memories rushed over him, as though they had only been waiting for the right word, the magic word, to free themselves from the unconscious. Before him he saw the old fir tree under which the boy had collected his treasures, and it seemed to him that he had left it only yesterday. He heard its deep and sheltering sough, and in the same second his heart was filled with the enigmatic music of the woods. Once he had taken part in the forests' primal life; fairy-tale beasts, trolls, and phantoms had been his company; and moss-covered stones and gray boulders, ages old, had given him murmuring instruction. His life had been filled by a familiarity and community with the things of nature, and in his eyes there had been no loneliness.

Where were his friends and protectors now? What crime

had he committed to make those who had been his intimates abandon him? How had he come to this place, to this musty room where all was strange and hateful to him?

Once again he had a painfully intense sensation of the loneliness which had held him in its grip since the morning. Strange old biblical sayings entered his thoughts, words which had stamped themselves into his memory during silent evenings when he lay in his little bed and father had not come home and mother sat in her rocking chair and read aloud from the New Testament; and he thought that everything they said was one and the same:

"Except a grain of wheat fall into the earth and die, it abideth by itself alone; but if it die, it beareth much fruit."

"He that findeth his life shall lose it; and he that loseth his life for my sake shall find it."

"I came that they may have life and may have it abundantly."

The little sculpture slipped from his hand, but he did not notice it. He took a few stumbling steps and, without knowing why he did it, left the room.

A comical little figure lay on the floor among the shavings.

When Myyriäinen went out onto the stoop, he noticed that it was springtime. After the long and bitter months the spring was suddenly there. Or was it only that he had not noticed it before? A shimmer lay over the poor roofs of the suburb, and there was a gentle dampness in the air, mixed with odd and muted rays of light, which aroused a yearning for a new life. The old poplar beside the military barracks sent out an odor at once pungent and benumbing. An old woman shambled along the street, muttering mysteriously to herself. Somewhere children were playing, and their shrill voices reached him like the cries of birds. Everything was so full of expression, everything came so very close to him that it seemed an invisible dividing wall between him and the world had fallen away. He felt like someone who leaves a prison and, shaken to the depths of his being, receives his first impressions of a living life. Suddenly all else appeared quite meaningless to him: his work, his mission, all save this one thing—to find some contact, to establish some communication. He hungered for a link with men and things the way a starved person hungers for food. Suddenly he perceived that he had gone around and around in the same circle all these years, had seen the same objects and made the same observations, without ever being able to break out of the ring, without ever seeing things in some new relationship.

He stood unmoving, like a statue, with his heavy body bent forward and his arms hanging down loosely at his sides; only the nervous sensitivity of his face and a secret fragility in his earth-bound form bore witness to the hidden activity of the spirit's forces.

He thought of his life and of how restricted and poverty-stricken it was, and of how much richer a form it could have taken. The world was full of beauty and there was always something new to see, if only the proper contact had been found. "Perhaps a person ought to venture out into the world," he thought. And he remembered all he had heard about the great cities in foreign lands where the holy treasures of art were preserved. In this springtime, too, the artists would make a pilgrimage to these places as to their true homeland. What lured them with such an irresistible force, what caused everyone who once had been there to long to return? Was it the new impressions which meant so much to them? But how were new impressions formed, after all? Weren't the connections which were revealed to one the important thing? Or the links which were joined and the communications which were established on paths that transcended the senses? For a moment he abandoned himself to the notion of making such a pilgrimage himself, in order to partake of these overflowing riches. But at the same time he knew that this way was not his own, and that he would never wander as a pilgrim to the holy cities of art. Here he thought less of his poverty and his ignorance and the other difficulties which could bar his path; instead he knew in his heart that he lacked that elasticity of intellect which makes a person set out into the world. His nature was rooted like the tree's; if the springs which nourished his soul ran dry, the only possibility that remained for him was to sink his roots still deeper into the earth from which he grew. "But I wonder if it's not tempting, just the same," he thought. "I'd rather make a pilgrimage to the fir tree of my childhood and to the wise old stones in my forest—if I could only find the way to them."

After this Myyriäinen did not touch his chisel or his knife again. He padded about quietly in his room, and his mother could only think that he was at work as usual. But now it was a different sort of work he had undertaken. It consisted for the most part in saying good-bye, in cutting small and delicate umbilical cords. He stored things away. He put everything in order. He himself was surprised to see how much there was to clean up after all these years—notes, half-finished sketches, half-erased memories, abandoned projects. But gradually it all got straightened out. The room grew neater every day that passed, and finally it stood spick and span, as if readied for a party. The tools had been left on the bench, but he had polished them, and rejoiced in seeing them lie side by side in perfect order. There is a gentle sadness about such tools.

There was something sad in his whole relationship to the

room. He had a sense of piety for what it contained. It seemed as though it had belonged to someone who was dead. He treated each object with gentle care. Nothing would be left to look after itself. He took care to see that each object regained the dignity it possesses in itself, when man does not use it carelessly. Painstakingly, he got his "old men" together and put them in a closet, where they could stand without being disturbed or without coming to harm in some other way.

While he poked around in the closet, he came upon a youthful work which he had all but forgotten. It was an early effort, made before he had even received the scanty training which had later come his way on various occasions. He felt a pain in his heart when he saw its head: its features were immortal, however clumsily they had been executed. No matter what: he felt that he must take a good look at this work, hidden long ago, before he locked it into the closet again. He went over to the window in order to examine it. Immediately he saw how inept and technically inferior it was, lacking any real unity or formal balance. But it was expressive just the same; there was something about it which moved him. There was a vision.

The word "Melancholy" had been carved into the base in big, angular letters. He sank into a contemplation of its care-laden features, and from the chaos of its ungainly lines the concept seemed to arise which he had had when the first sketch came into being. He beheld the poet's head in the shadow of melancholy's dark wings: the forehead's mighty vault above the broken lines of the face and the mouth, lines broken by pain, the head bent forward as though to listen to the sad songs and savage ballads of the people. It was like a shell in which the people's heart reverberated as the ocean does. In its loneliness, the land of winter and forests had brought forth this head, and on its forehead there stood written: this is my most beloved son. An outsider, perhaps, could see nothing of this in the clumsily carved head, still another reason why he had never shown it to anyone, but rather had left it lying in its place of concealment. But as for himself, he could not behold it again without being overwhelmed by the beauty of the image as he had dreamed it. In some manner, despite everything, the beauty remained, like a hint or a careless notation, and that alone, he thought, was worth more than all the carefully worked-out little figures he had finished later on.

The rhythm of the world's most wondrous cradle-song echoed in his ears. It was melancholy's own song, and it streamed toward him from the poet's forehead:

> Grove of death and grove nocturnal!
> There's a fine and sandy cradle,
> Thither shall I lead my baby.*

He was seized by an unfathomable tenderness of which he did not know whether it bore death or life in its embrace, whether it sought the last extreme of loneliness or the deepest community. Groping and gentle, his hand passed over this head which he had once begot in a dream, and the memory of the moment of conception swept over him like a hot wave, and he could feel how he had emptied his soul in a mystical union with the primal image he had beheld. He had emptied himself until he reached the boundaries of nothingness and a fullness had filled him unto overflowing. "This is the secret of art," a voice within him said. "This is the secret of love and of death."

Afterwards he would remember this moment as the one in which he for the first time grasped something of the mystery of death.

* Hagar Olsson quotes from the Finnish text of a poem included in *The Seven Brothers:* "Tuonen lehto, öinen lehto! / Siell on hieno hietakehto, / Sinnepä lapseni saatan."—*Translator's note.*

With a feeling of relief and satisfaction he looked into the closet where he had put his neat little men. But he did not put back the poet's head. He kept it for himself.

Next morning at the rising of the sun he awakened from a dream. He felt that sensation of deep rest which one knows when one has slumbered a while on a soft granite cliff and listened to the sound of the woods and the sea. He took a deep breath, lifted himself up on his elbow, and looked out. He saw that the sun had just risen; it sent its first warm tones of gold into the milky, unreal light of the summer night. It could not have been more than about three o'clock. He lay back again and closed his eyes, drawn to his fleeing dream-world's incomprehensible joy.

He sank into a quiet doze. The dream which had vanished upon his awakening returned, in fragments, only to be erased again in some magic way. A single picture remained, broken loose from a background which had been washed away by the river of forgetfulness; perhaps it was on this account that it exerted such a mysterious attraction, just as a half-solved riddle does. He saw a road which he thought he recognized, although he could not remember where he had seen it, and in the middle of the road there stood a lone and quite extraordinary man. He appeared to be familiar, yet was disturbingly strange. He looked like a tramp; he was dark and had a long stubble, his clothes were dishevelled, and he wore his cap pulled down over his eyes, the way people do in this part of the country. From beneath his closed eyelids, Myyriäinen regarded him with intense interest, and slowly he was filled with the deep joy his dream had given him. Really: the odd thing about the man was that he stood staring at someone who Myyriäinen finally realized had to be himself. "Why are you staring at me that way?" said Myyriäinen. And in the same moment he was wide awake. He realized that it was Jesus. Jesus stood in the middle of the road gazing meaningfully at Myyriäinen, who had had no contact with Him or even heard His name mentioned since he was a child. He was not in the least surprised that Jesus looked the way he did, unshaven, seedy, worn out from deprivation and a vagrant's life. It was all the more overwhelming because one knew immediately it was Jesus. "That's how the Son of Man looks," he thought fleetingly.

He closed his eyes and made himself comfortable in the feeling that, for the first time in his life, something supernatural had touched him, like a hand which reaches out and touches one's shoulder. The last thing he saw before he went to sleep again on his granite slab was the look in that raised and ravaged head, which said to him with all the power of its mild and flaming countenance: "Arise and leave all that you have at hand!"

Two: Departure

Who knows the magic of these regions, lost in their dreams? We who lived among this folk as outsiders have been bewildered to see its enigmatic treasures neglected and unsung, even ridiculed, while an alien spirit asserted itself and claimed victor's right to the weakly defended sanctuaries. In the distant quiet villages on the shore of the holy lake, where so much blood flowed and fire raged for Christ's sake, the people have concealed their treasures in the earth, and there someday a poet will perhaps find the five-stringed kantele between moss-grown graves and rotting sacred images.

The roads, bright with summer, gave a friendly welcome to the prodigal son. Myyriäinen entered with all his soul into this landscape which had bestowed upon its children so much of its own generosity and softness, its wealth of shades, its magical intensity, and which even in the depth of his own reserved and heavy nature guarded a fragment of its indestructible treasure, the dreamer's gift. He was at home here; at every turn in the road and at every flower-covered and stony hillside his childhood's landscape offered him inexhaustible sources of joy. From behind his pale blue eyes there looked out a secret nature avidly appeasing its hunger upon things, lights, moods which only a deeply kindred spirit can absorb. What does man live by? The wise and the mighty of this world do not know, but a Myyriäinen, drawing deep breaths in the middle of a sun-warmed road, knows in a fleeting second that he lives by joy and joy alone. If someone should ever get the idea of using joy as a measure of whatever is worth striving after in life, then perhaps the reflections of light on an old fence post where a crow is sitting, or the ominous rattle of leaves on an evening late in autumn, would have a high value, and perhaps even the philosophers would understand why the experiences of childhood possess a worth before which so much of what seems important in life grows pale.

Here Myyriäinen walked his childhood's golden ways. The gray, moss-covered fences along the roads, the poor gray settlements, as if from the Stone Age, on the hillocks, the potato patches and the sweet-smelling hops and the clear-eyed bells of the flowers and the flaxen-haired children playing gravely beside the sauna—all this filled him with a happiness which nothing else in the world could have given him, and the wild softness of the broad heather-grown moors caressed him with the tender hands of an old nurse.

Each time he adjusted his knapsack he felt the pressure of a hard object jutting against his shoulder blade. It was the poet's head which he had stuffed in at the last minute, when he had already finished packing. He had not thought of it before. His sole idea had been to get started as soon as he awoke the next morning. He quickly saw that his room had in reality already been abandoned. It stood lost, as it were, in its own repose, not waiting to be taken possession of by some busy spirit. Everything was in its proper place. Everything was in order. All that remained for him was to arise and go. Without the slightest hesitation he took out his green knapsack which had been his faithful companion during all the years he had carried around his funny old men to their prospective buyers. He filled the knapsack with his modest personal possessions; even when taking leave of most of one's possessions, there are still a few things one wants to take along. He moved quite lightly now, almost floating, with a soft sureness which otherwise was foreign to his clumsy form. On his forehead and cheeks there lay a pale flush which betrayed that his heart beat more rapidly than it was accustomed, a flush which gave his hollow grayish face an almost comically childish air. He began to whistle without knowing it, something he had not done since he was a boy and tended his flock in the forest; and perhaps he already felt the soft tussocks of the woods bending beneath his feet, and felt the tall trees stretching their branches out over him in a gesture of majestic protection.

He was about to tie his knapsack shut when he caught sight of the poet's head. Once again he was fascinated by its sorrowful expression. Standing beside his pack, he stared at the carving. Perhaps it happened because in his present condition he was so little receptive to concrete visual impressions; but he plainly saw another face emerge from the familiar features, the same worn-out face he had seen in the dream, and the divine eyes looked straight into his. He saw the road where the solitary figure had appeared, and now he suddenly recognized it. It was a piece of his childhood's road, between his home and the village, just at the bend beside the big Witch's Stone (he used to call it that because it looked as if it could swallow up little children in its rough and mossy maws, with their ugly teeth of white lichen) and the magically twisted old pine which he loved and felt sorry for, because it had grown fast-joined to the stone and yet kept up such a friendly soughing in its noble crown. As vividly as if he were indeed watching, he saw himself as a little bare-legged boy who ran panting along the road with his birch-bark satchel on his back.

He hastily stuffed the poet's head into his sack, and if

there had not been enough room inside, then he would have taken out something else to make a place for it.

Just when everything was ready and he stood testing his pack with his hand, his mother appeared in the door. He stood with his back to her, but still he saw her as plainly as in a revelation, her right hand propped against the doorpost and her left pressed against her heart, while her tired gray glance rallied itself to meet the inevitable. Perhaps she had heard him whistling, perhaps she knew what was about to happen without this warning. When he looked at her, she merely nodded and returned to the kitchen.

She sank down heavily beside the table and let him pour the coffee. She did not say a word, and he said nothing either. They were not accustomed to dress their innermost thoughts in words. The old woman muttered to herself as she usually did when they were at the table, and he sat as he usually did, leaning forward, with his arms in his lap and his glance withdrawn. After a time he got up, made an awkward and rather shy bow in his mother's direction, as he was wont to do in order to thank her for the food, and then took hold of his knapsack. As he tossed it over his shoulder he said, without turning around toward her: "I'm going on a trip for a while now." His mother answered: "I can see that." Nothing more was said between them.

But when he had closed the door and begun his journey toward that land whither his longing led him, he talked long and profoundly with the old woman who had been left alone in the house. After all, she was the only person in the whole world who was near to him, and he had much to tell her concerning life and a little boy with a birch-bark satchel on his back.

He did not choose his course as a result of any deliberations. It unfolded all by itself. Naturally, he knew that he had to go toward the east, to those reaches where he had his home, and he needed to know no more. His home-parish up in the north did not lie in his thoughts, nor would he ever get that far on his journey. But wherever he went, his childhood followed him like an invisible companion. Memories from early years joined him and kept him company as he wandered along the broad and busy highway, hearing the hum of the cars and the rattle of the carts and the wagoners' shouts as a distant roaring in his ears.

One day, in the middle of the busiest hour, when he had been under way since the rising of the sun and was looking around, exhausted, for a shady place to rest, the awful memory of the suicide's autopsy suddenly rose up from the oblivion where it had lain hidden. He could no longer tell whether he had actually had the chance to see the suicide's face during that hideous process, which he had sneaked in to watch together with some other boys, or whether afterwards, in his excited condition, he had dreamed of it. But in this moment he plainly saw the swollen face which had a ghastly blue color, and he felt the shudder of disgust and pleasure which had assailed the boy when his ugly curiosity had been satisfied. He recalled that his imagination and the other children's had revolved for a long time around the "suicide," with an unnatural inquisitiveness which could only be compared to the excitement which seized them when they beheld certain other events they were not supposed to witness. "He can't be buried in consecrated earth," they whispered to one another in their excitement, and this phrase had an incomprehensible ability to awaken dismay and terror. It was as though the little savages, not guessing what really transpired, experienced the magical import of age-old conceptions of death with an intensity, bordering on ecstasy, to which adults no longer had access, although their mental world was essentially the same. "What can it be," Myyriäinen wondered, "which makes the popular imagination separate the suicide in such a hideous way from the man who dies a normal death? Isn't there some connection here with a deep comprehension of death's sanctity, of the holy import of dying?"

He was so lost in his thoughts that he neglected to look for a place to rest in the shade. Life's hasty movement marched past on the sun-baked highway, men toiled with sweaty faces and bent backs for their daily bread; he proceeded as in a dream. Abruptly, another memory from his childhood appeared, as much unlike its predecessor as the day is unlike the night, and yet secretly connected to it. It was a small, small flame which burned unchangingly and quietly in a human dwelling place. At first he only saw the little flame; then there emerged the weakly illuminated icon beneath which it burned, and the dark corner where the logs of the wall were blackened to ebony's dusky shine. Finally he saw the whole cottage. It was so small and low that it seemed made for dwarfs to dwell in; it had a window so tiny that a child's face, pressed against the pane, filled it entirely. He himself sat on the bench, his nose running, hungry, in despair; he had run away from home, bare-legged and wearing only a few ragged clothes, in the midst of the winter's worst cold. He sat quietly on the bench, his aching legs drawn up beneath him, and did nothing but gaze at the little flame with a shimmer of happiness upon his face. Roaring, the snowstorm passed over the roof, and the beasts of the forest hid themselves trembling in their lairs, but the little flame, unchanging and still, burned in its corner, as though it belonged to another world.

Myyriäinen stopped for a moment in the middle of the highway and closed his eyes in order to be better able to see; it was a miracle that he did not fall victim to an accident. Perhaps his kind little dwarf-woman protected him. She treated him like a prince and let the bounties of a fairy tale fall to his lot, beautiful rich-smelling *piroshki* and steaming coffee, and when he asked her what was burning so brightly over there in the corner, she answered that it was Our Savior's heart. "No one loves us poor people except Him," she said, and put a friendly hand on his head. Now he remembered everything with perfect clarity, and he could not understand how he had ever forgotten it. He knew of course that the little light had made a deep impression on him, because he had never seen anything like it before; the woman came from outside their parish, and was perhaps the only person in the whole region who professed the old faith. And perhaps he was also in special need of the supernatural's mild protection at that time. But wasn't there something else too? He remembered how often he had made his way to the hut later on, in the greatest secrecy, as though it were something he wanted to keep to himself; and if the old woman was not at home or if she was asleep, he pressed his nose flat against the pane in order at least to get a glimpse of the little flame. As small as he was, he imagined how pretty it would be with the little flame in the room, when the old woman lay there all alone and dead. He often thought of the old woman lying dead in her cottage; the flame seemed to talk, forever and unchangingly, about something which was connected with her death.

This series of images, arising one after the other from a sort of secret and forgotten storeroom, was so vivid that he got the impression that the little flame beneath the dwarf-woman's icon illuminated by its feeble light a whole world of unknown knowledge within him. "Longing dwells within it," he thought. And he came to reflect that, if he knew so little of what dwelt in his innermost being, how much the less he knew of what went on within this people from whom he had sprung, and from whom he had somehow become estranged. What did he know of its innermost and dream-veiled secrets?

All at once he realized that here he entered a culture which, in an essential and decisive way, was directed toward the East, which still stood in living contact with impulses from distant and duskily illuminated centuries, when crusaders from Novgorod and holy men from Athos had implanted the light of Christianity in the people's heart, long before the West came to these reaches with fire and sword. He thought that just as he had preserved the memory of the little flame through the decades, so this people had concealed the flame of the naive faith within their hearts, and in all secrecy; and whoever did not realize it was a stranger here, and ought never to enter this land.

Many thought they were familiar with this responsive, cheerful, quick-eyed folk, but if one could penetrate to its innermost being and listen to the deepest springs which were concealed from the stranger with craft and cunning, one might perhaps get to hear sounds which had not been heard since the kantele fell silent and the people's song grew dumb. Why had it become so still in these groves? Why had the song grown silent? He looked around, as if he expected to hear Marjatta's song or the Old One's music * coming from the nearby stand of birch trees. What a magic and familiar peace, the peace of the wilderness, lay upon this little glade in the forest! He stopped, spellbound: this was in truth the land of song. The earth itself was song, the hillocks' soft rhythm was song, the catkins of the weeping birch were song. The landscape had acquired another tone, more mysterious and more spiritual. It was no longer just his childhood's landscape, it was something else and something more, it was the virgin land where his people had found its soul and where his own yearning had its primal home.

Myyriäinen had wandered through many parishes and sat on many benches, worn shiny with use, in old-fashioned

* Marjatta, the Virgin Mary, is the subject of the 50th Canto of the *Kalevala;* the "Old One" is Väinämöinen, the chief figure in the epic.—*Translator's note.*

cottages that swarmed with children, when circumstances decreed that he should make the acquaintance of his prospective friend and benefactor, Iivana Lampinen, the tinker from our village. The one who stopped him at the right moment was an ill-tempered old man with a white beard, who early one morning in June sat by the wayside talking to himself. He looked like a prophet from the Old Testament, and Myyriäinen could not keep from going up and saying hello to him. When the old man discovered that he had a listener, he immediately exploded into passionate curses; trembling, he waved his clenched fists in the air and called down calamity onto the heads of his own children. They had driven their father out of house and home, may every ill descend upon them, may God strike them with pestilences and evil eyes! A peculiar and primitive magnificence lay upon the old man's gestures, and his speech had a strength and a fire which could have befitted King Lear. Myyriäinen listened fascinated to his confused litany. He reflected that revenge must be the mightiest of the spirits of the earth; what a triumph it celebrated over the old man's fragility, his actual impotence!

He had hardly brought his thought to an end before his attention was captured by a curious cortege which came along the road at a sharp trot. He got a confused impression of some strange black figures and pale flowing manes, and almost immediately found himself in the midst of an indescribable chaos. Not until afterwards was he able to figure out that the lead horse had shied away from his prophet, who stood with his hands raised in malediction; the cart had turned over and its passengers had landed in the ditch. The first detail which he clearly perceived was a tall, crepe-hung, black hat which lay badly battered in the ditch. He stared at it for a long time, as if he thought it unnatural that such an item had suddenly appeared among the nettles and the coltsfoot in a ditch beside a Finnish highway. Slowly he realized that he was looking at the head-covering of an Orthodox priest-monk.

The monks and the peasants from all of the four carts stood together in a flock, staring as though frozen at a monk who lay on the edge of the ditch in a twisted position, his face turned upward. A peaceful composure which resembled that of death lay spread over his pale countenance. Myyriäinen could not take his eyes away from it. He felt someone touch him, but in order not to lose the expression in the monk's face, he did not turn around to see who it was. He merely heard the knowing voice which said: "Very likely the monk is dead now."

To his astonishment he saw the angry prophet press his way past the others and throw himself down on the ground. "Mercy, father, mercy! Have pity on a poor sinner," he cried with the same passionate voice in which he had recently hurled his curses. He wept aloud in awareness of his guilt, and Myyriäinen marveled in his heart at these tears which came rushing forth from a ground as hard as stone. The company grew mightily excited; everyone shouted at the same time, pointing at the poor old man who had been the cause of the accident. A red-faced peasant was just about to kick him out of the way with his boot-clad foot when the supposed dead man arose, as much unharmed as if he had rested on the wings of angels. He gazed at the confused faces around him and reproached himself for not having been able to lift these others, by his ardor's hidden might, to the region of peace where he himself had tarried. When the accident occurred, he had closed his eyes, collected his spirit, and descended into the measureless depths of prayer's serenity. He had lain unmoving, just as he had been cast to the ground, until a prayer for pity had reached his distant ear. "Go in peace, my son. Your sin is not greater than mine, and Our Savior lives," he said with the oddly veiled and yet shining voice of him who returns. The impression of these simple words, ringing through dark discords with the pure and silver note of spiritual deliberation, was so strong that all the people present, the monks as well as the peasants, fell as one man to their knees, bowing to the earth before an invisible majesty.

Abel Myyriäinen was the only person present who did not fall to his knees on this occasion; someone who has Lutheran obstinacy in his blood and has been trained to be insensitive toward symbolic actions cannot do such things. But the event made a strong impression upon him. He had received an insight into the relation of the Orthodox church to the people, and he was astonished at how easily and unpretentiously the transcendental joined itself to the natural and the prosaic. He gazed fixedly at the monk's white face with the shining eyes and the jet-black, well-tended beard which gave the countenance a stern and ascetic air. He did not know who stood before him, but the secret reverence he felt told him that he had entered into contact with a spiritual force to which he had never paid heed before.

Later he would find out that it was Father Isaakij he had met, the priest-monk from the secluded little cloister on the lonely island, a man known in the whole of the Orthodox world as one of the great heroes of "unceasing prayer." His seemingly unimportant cloister, consecrated to the memory of the birth of the Mother of God, for centuries had been a citadel of prayer and intercession, from which beams of quiet light had gone out to the people of these marches, devastated by unrest and war.

Three: Meeting with Death

"Those monks," Myyriäinen thought, "are great artists, no question about it. They ought to be able to teach a man something about the real nature of art."

Musing, he gazed after the four carts which had disappeared in a cloud of dust, bound in the direction of the village he himself had left a couple of hours before. The monks most likely were going to call on some esteemed fellow-believers in the neighborhood. In the evening they would return to their cloister. It was not very far from here, he knew that much. But it was not a cloister which one visited for amusement's sake. Mindful of the secularization which had taken place in the region's large and more famous brother-house, the abbot here had declared that he wished no guests save those who came for edification and to invoke the aid of the miracle-working Madonna, the cloister's most precious icon. And Myyriäinen knew in his heart that, no matter how much he wanted to strip away his former self, he could not become a pilgrim in spirit and in truth. The holy rites would say nothing to him, and the wonderful hymns would only leave a fleeting impression of beauty.

It bothered him that the little man with the knowing voice who had spoken to him a while ago during the general uproar would not leave him in peace now. Bursting with meaning, he stood beneath a birch tree at the very roadside and waved eagerly; there was a handcart a short distance from him. Perhaps he wanted to sell him something. The man's appearance was amusing: he wore drooping trousers and had a cornflower stuck elegantly into the buttonhole of his coat. He had a benign grin all over his face and winked his eyes cunningly; he looked as if he had some trick or other up his sleeve.

Myyriäinen shook his head and decided not to pay the man any attention. He would simply continue his journey, and get rid of him that way. But it went against his grain to leave this place without any further ado: so many strange thoughts had come to him here. He looked ahead with a certain sadness. He could see the little turn-off a few hundred meters along the road; this was where the monks had come from, as far as he could tell. In all likelihood, the turn-off led only to the monks' jetty down at the water's edge. Perhaps some sort of settlement was there, too. But he had no reason to go that way. It led nowhere.

While he stood there in his indecision, trying to keep from looking at the little man and his irritating signals, his thoughts continued to spin their unending thread. Meanwhile, full of attention, the man came forward and introduced himself: "Iivana Lampinen," he said with an extremely well-mannered, almost courtly bow. Without taking the time to wait for an answer, he doused the stranger in a torrent of benign words. It was a fine day under God's heaven, and nice to meet this way on the highway of life, and couldn't he offer the stranger some *piroshki* and fresh butter, Palaga really had a way with *piroshki*, and who knows when we'll meet again in the marketplace of life? Myyriäinen gave what he thought might be an appropriate answer, and after repeated promptings and friendly shoves he let himself be dragged along to the resting-place beneath the birch tree, where a pile of greasy pastry and a tub of yellow butter could be seen shining from afar. He sat down in the grass and ate heartily and listened with half an ear to Lampinen's good-natured chatter. But his thoughts continued to spin their endless thread undisturbed. . . .

"All the same, it's strange that people have thought up the idea of God. And then they've built these shining temples and richly ornamented cloisters all over the world's surface, and created tones and colors and shapes of incomprehensible beauty in order to express His being. Has man sought a reflection of the divine beauty in his own works? But who can say that beauty is not an illusion? Instead, is it possible that man glorifies himself in this beauty? Why should God be beautiful? He can just as well be hideous, the way the idols of primitive peoples are. He is nothing of all these things which we can imagine. He is that strange, that completely different something which no living person has beheld. Perhaps we conceal it in beauty in order that we may protect ourselves from it. Perhaps those monks are charlatans after all. . . ."

Feeling confused, he opened his eyes. He noticed that he lay beneath a birch tree, listening to an old and monotonous recitation. He remembered that he had eaten here together with someone called Lampinen, and perhaps he had fallen asleep for a while after the meal. A passing thought told him that it must be Lampinen who was reciting something in this curious, half-singing fashion. But he did not take the trouble to raise himself up, he did not even lift his head. He simply lay there, listening, and as the monotonous rhythm carried the words to him, he felt that his body rose lightly and almost imperceptibly from the ground, and hovered unsupported in the air, in harmony with the soft and solemn movements of the earth and of the other heavenly bodies:

> Lull the child, oh Lord in heaven,
> lull it, heavenly Maria,
> even I perhaps could slumber,
> could I be but briefly idle.
>
> Sleep, come to the baby's cradle,
> dream, come softly to the bedstead,
> where the little child is lying
> sweet and still beneath the cover,
> let the little baby slumber,
> see how its frail strength is waning,
> let it like the earth lie restful,
> let it dream like tree and meadow,
> let it have fair dreams, Maria,
> give it of your holy quiet.

He could hear that Lampinen had finished his song, and in its stead talked quietly with someone who did not want to go to sleep. But he did not move. The song continued to sing within him. The tones darkened, the melody grew more and more lonely, and still the song remained the same. It was the song of Tuoni's land * and of the Maid of Death who lulls her child to rest at eventide. Perhaps the poet had found the song on the lips of the people and had turned it into a cradlesong for his own lonesome heart. His listening head was like a shell which echoed with the songs of the people. Myyriäinen thought that the head must be still more beautiful than it had appeared to his eyes. And suddenly he could

* In Myyriäinen's mind, the folksong sung by Lampinen is transformed into the poem of Kivi, quoted in the first chapter.—*Translator's note.*

not understand why he had ever doubted the absolute and indivisible beauty of God.

"There is a hidden music in everything which stands close to God," he thought. "One must have an ear to capture this music, and not be led astray. The simple folksong and great and lonely men possess the same music. Those who have shaken the dust of their suffering from their feet stand close to God."

Very gently, someone touched his shoulder, and to his surprise he saw that a thin little arm lay on his breast, and that a child bent over him and peered at him searchingly. His friend Lampinen held the girl in his arms, and, in order that the child could touch him, Lampinen had got down on his knees beside him.

"Sanni wanted so much to greet our guest," Lampinen said with a broad grin. "She's excited now, you see, and doesn't want to go to sleep, since we shall be at the house of God's Mother in a little while."

Looking at the little group, Myyriäinen felt ashamed. He had been so busy with his own thoughts that he had completely forgotten his fellow traveler. And what on earth had kept him from noticing the girl? She must have been the gray bundle he had thought he saw lying on the handcart.

"Why didn't you come over and say hello to me, I'm the oldest daughter of Iivana Lampinen," the girl said in a voice eager and a little shrill, which she had difficulty in controlling. She breathed in short gasps, and when Myyriäinen got a better look at her, he realized that she was very ill, perhaps even close to death. It was not just because she was emaciated and unnaturally pale, or because the hair that fell over her forehead was sticky with sweat; the whole of her little face with its sunken eyes was secretly marked by the brush of death, which paints shadows and draws lines of expression in its own strange and unfamiliar way.

"I thought you were asleep," Myyriäinen answered in order to excuse himself.

"You shouldn't believe what Lampinen says, he's just telling stories," the girl said in her shrillest voice. She continued to talk with an unnatural exaltation, and even though Myyriäinen could tell very well how much of an effort it cost her, he did not have the heart to interrupt her or to make any movement which could have disturbed her. He knew instinctively that it was necessary for the girl to speak her mind; she had to hear her own exposition of things in order to find a connection with that life which, in some curious fashion, threatened to dissolve into mists, to disappear beyond her grasp.

She bent over him with a mysterious expression.

"I'm not supposed to sleep, you see, it's absolutely necessary for me not to sleep. Lampinen is so childish, he doesn't understand what's going on. It's dangerous to sleep when you're sick, for it's happened that some people don't wake up at all, and then they say you're dead and stuff you into the ground. Then you can't do anything, I'm sure you realize that. And who would take care of Lampinen's children then? There's nobody to clean up and sweep the floor and look after baby brother, Palaga Lampinen won't do that, she never will, and Mikko—he hasn't learned to walk yet—will do his business under him if I'm not there to carry him outside. Because Asser, you know, goes to school and all kinds of places and they won't get him to do womenfolk's work. He was supposed to carry in the water last winter, Lampinen ordered him to, but I had to bring up every last bucket myself, and Asser took the shoes I got from Mrs. Mitronen and I've never had them on a single time and Palaga Lampinen just laughed and said that a man's a man even in short trousers. Now you can see why it would be terribly unlucky if I happened to fall asleep and didn't know what was happening. Of course, the worst is that you can't depend on Lampinen. It's too bad that God's Mother has to live so far away that I'm not able to walk there all by myself. I'm glad you're coming along, because then you can keep an eye on Lampinen, you never know what he can think up, and then you'll see to it that I don't go to sleep, promise me that, please promise me."

The girl grabbed his lapel with a strength that astonished him and looked him straight in the eyes with an unnaturally dilated gaze; he felt a stab of pain to see how her glance first grew clouded and then was quickly extinguished, as if this last effort had broken her exhausted soul's power to resist. Her head drooped, and the struggling spark of life was plunged into dull sleep.

Lampinen got up carefully from his kneeling position, nodded encouragingly to Myyriäinen, and went off to put the girl to bed on the handcart. He walked as lightly and lithely as an Indian; his trousers hung in indescribable folds, and the heavy fur cap which he wore despite the summer's warmth gave the skinny little figure a certain melancholy dignity.

Myyriäinen had sat up; he followed Lampinen's movements with his eyes. Now he knew exactly what Sanni's case was: a child who had never been allowed to be a child, who at the age of ten already had a woman's burdensome life behind her. He was thoroughly familiar with such situations. It was the oldest girl's customary lot in the poor cottages of this region, where a child was born just about every year, and where the mother had to work outside. Undernourished, without enough clothes to go outside in the winter, grown crooked from constantly holding a baby too heavy for her strength, bound like a prisoner to the cradle and the musty-smelling hearth—that was little Sanni and her life. What shook him in her comments was her touching officiousness. She was so breathlessly eager and fussy that anyone could tell she was indispensable. All her duties and everything she had had to bear were put on display—not in order to complain but rather to show how indispensable she was, and how necessary it was for that dark power to fail in its plan of making her an outsider, as if she were someone who could be done without. The very fact of her life's absolute misery made her fate especially moving. He remembered how often people are heard to say that death would be a blessing for such wretched creatures as Sanni. It was true that her life had been hard and more burdensome than any human being's, let alone a child's, ought to be, but she herself knew that it had borne a profit just the same, something the value of which she alone could really understand. She did not wish to surrender this poor treasure.

Lampinen stored away the little gray bundle with great care. It was very amusing to watch him. His otherwise happy-go-lucky manner acquired a certain resolute and motherly quality when he fussed over the girl. He no doubt recalled the determined movements Palaga Lampinen used when she swaddled her infants, hard and tight, so that the little creature would have some stability in its existence and not get the chance to do itself harm. Thus he went to work with a will, taking pains to see that everything was made as taut as possible.

Myyriäinen sat thinking of Sanni's little hands. They lay all feeble and spent beneath their coverlets, while the transcendent heart sent up messages for help to unknown protectors. An oppressive sense of powerlessness came upon him. He knew—he had known it ever since he first saw the girl—that every hope was gone and that the officious little hands would never return to their world. They would disappear from it as if they had never been there; and everything would continue as it had before. Suddenly he realized what it was that threatened the girl and what she tried to defend herself against with her naive officiousness. It was not death at all, this dark melody which he had so often thought he heard in his dreams, like an undertone in everything which was and everything which would be. Why should death be so frightening? Why should he have felt this icy breath in his soul, merely because a poverty-stricken child he had met on the highway was going to die? He had seen many people die and kept his self-composure, and he lived in an age which, as though strangely drunk with death, prepared to offer its hecatombs on death's altar. And he had never been able to feel anything save a vague weight upon his soul and at the same time a dream-like enticement, a need to partake, himself, of these dark sacrificial rites, a need to achieve knowledge of their secret import. No, it was not death at all that frightened him. It was not the shadow of death he saw in little Sanni's wide-open eyes. It was the shadow of Nothingness—that everything had been without meaning and that little Sanni's "death" would be as senseless as her "life."

A chill ran through him, as though the sun had disappeared and the earth emanated an icy breath born of Nothingness itself. It seemed that he had chanced upon a land of vapors where every signpost vanishes and the solid ground beneath man's foot gives way in misty unreality. He had a fleeting notion that it was anguish over this which made men hurl themselves toward death in hope of being saved from simply succumbing to it.

In this hour he might perhaps have fallen prey to one of those mysterious and fateful spiritual catastrophes which for some reason may lay waste the lives of men, without their having the slightest idea of what caused the collapse, if he had been left to himself and had not had contact with some friendly-minded being. But Iivana Lampinen was not the man to let a chance for human fellowship escape him. He approached Myyriäinen and stood before him, looking at him with his head on one side and a cunning gleam in the corner of his eye.

"You'd better come along," he said. "Sanni would dearly love it. And then, of course, it will be a little more solemn that way."

Myyriäinen was almost frightened. Should he join the pilgrimage to the miracle-working madonna? He already knew that the girl would die. And what sense was there in it? He could not seriously believe in a miracle. If he went along, his conviction that Sanni must die would be written all over him, and that really wasn't fair play, somehow.

Lampinen was not embarrassed by his failure to get an answer. He stood with his hands in his pockets, peering up at the sky. This was his way of telling time, and besides, it was pleasant for a person with the gift of fantasy to lose himself in the contemplation of the heavens' blue arch. One could tell how much at home he was when he stood free as a bird on the wooded hillside, with the open highway before him. The nonchalance of his person, slovenly and a little tarnished, never appeared to better advantage than in such a moment. His shoulders were not loaded with any invisible burdens. The light and restless clouds of early summer floated above his shabby fur cap.

"It's getting on toward the time to start out now," he said thoughtfully. It was an announcement of the most general nature, intended to begin a conversation in a discreet sort of way. After such an observation, nothing can be more agreeable than embarking upon vague and generally valid reflections which have the advantage that in an ingenious and delightful manner they heighten the pleasure of postponing whatever it is one intends to do.

But Myyriäinen had other things to think of. He did not take his eyes from the bundle on Lampinen's cart. There, life was gathering for the last great test of strength.

"Sanni doesn't have much time left," he said quickly, as if he wanted to get it said once and for all. But straightway he became conscious of the impropriety of his remark: it is not fitting for one person to reckon in advance with another's death.

To his surprise he heard Lampinen chuckle with delight.

"Of course! That's exactly what I told Palaga. It's a sickness unto death, mark my words, I said. But don't think she bothers to listen to what somebody else says. She just laughs and won't hear a word of anything that doesn't suit her. She's always been that way, you see. Lots of times it's really funny, I'll tell you. But Iivana Lampinen recognizes the signs. He knows exactly when somebody's about to die. And if the person's got a reprieve, you can tell that by looking at him, too, no matter how badly off he is."

Myyriäinen got up, tormented by what he had heard. He thought he could not breathe. He went over to the girl, stationing himself beside her cart in a vague feeling that he had to protect her.

"In my opinion, you shouldn't make a pilgrimage to the Mother of God," he said to Lampinen. "You don't have the proper faith."

Troubled, Lampinen rubbed his nose; he could not quite understand what Myyriäinen was talking about.

"That may be right," he said with his customary ready compliance. "A poor devil could certainly have other things to do. But remember—a father's heart. I've always had a soft spot for the children, you see. And when Sanni got the idea in her head . . . Mitronen's daughter Alvina visited us one evening and babbled on and on about the Most Holy image which is supposed to be in the cloister, and which is supposed to be so holy that all kinds of illnesses leave a person like an evil breath, if he can just get the chance to touch the image and pronounce his own name the way it's written in the church register. Why, Sanni was absolutely transformed when she heard about it. You couldn't recognize her. She begged and pleaded, and you didn't have the heart to watch it burning in her eyes night and day. After all, a person doesn't die more than once in his life, and so you can act a little extravagantly, if that's the way it has to be. Of course, Palaga wouldn't hear of it. To tell the truth, she has trouble doing without her husband. But I said what I believe—that the girl wouldn't find any rest in her grave if she died without getting to touch the Most Holy image. She'll come back as a ghost, I said, and then Palaga's face turned white as a sheet and she didn't know what to do. That evening she took care of that poor little creature of a Sanni as if a count's child had landed in our house, and she told the children to keep quiet. No matter how you look at it, there's something special about a person who's going to die. And you can just as well put yourself out a little."

Lampinen could go on croaking about death as much as he wanted to, it didn't concern Myyriäinen. He experienced one of those moments when life's innermost heart seems to open up before the eyes of men, and they sink into that all-reconciling bliss which flows out steadily and without end. A bolt of light had penetrated the labyrinth of conceptions of death in which he had been groping. In his mind he saw the little girl in utter reality, lying on the bench by the oven at home, quite alone, abandoned by the living, counted among the dead. A blush flamed up in her pale cheeks, a fire was kindled deep within her tired eyes, her glance grew large, and suddenly she saw that God's Mother would make her whole. It was no more remarkable than what took place in a creative imagination when the projected work emerged in its first and transcendent form. It was no more remarkable, and it was equally remarkable: inspiration, the eternal miracle. If the girl had not been chosen and called by this first miracle, she would never have embraced the thought of the pilgrimage to God's Mother in Her cloister with the mysterious, inexorable tenacity of purpose which at last overcame all opposition. She might have listened to what Mitronen's daughter Alvina said, just as he would have listened to it, without paying it more attention than any other story. But she knew as soon as she heard it that it was meant for her and no one else, that she was the one who would touch the image and utter her name in the presence of the Mother of God.

Myyriäinen heard a bird singing close to him. It sang with such an intoxicating zeal and shrillness that it seemed it would rather burst its throat than cease the expression of its feelings. The clear high tones stumbled over one another in their infinite eagerness, filling the air with a jubilation like that we would know if the flowers and the trees opened a thousand mute mouths, and yet it was just a single little bird which sang the praises of the day. He listened, strangely spellbound, as if it were the first time in his life he had perceived the miracle in a chaffinch's song.

He could hear Lampinen telling some interesting detail about that same Alvina, Mitronen's daughter, but it did not concern him. He bent down over the unconscious girl and looked at the closed little face which emerged from among the rags.

"A human face is a strange thing, all the same," he thought. "There's something in it you don't see at the first glance." He reflected for a while on what it could be in such a little face which was so hard to reach. He came to think of those old jugs which are dug up from the earth and which have shape and color of a sort that no living man has ever seen, and which no one can imitate.

"Actually it's all very simple, although you have trouble in understanding it. After all, there's only one Sanni among all the people who live and who have lived on the face of the earth. And there will never be someone else who is Sanni. In her way, Sanni realizes that. She knows it in her heart. Thus she certainly has the right—if anybody does—to a fate which isn't like other people's. If she agrees to die, then there has to be some meaning in it, maybe a sad meaning, but a meaning in any case. And little Sanni's death can't have any meaning at all, if there weren't some meaning in her life. Sanni knows all of this in her own way, and that's why she's making her life's great journey now."

He was ready to join the pilgrims without hesitation. He had a dim notion that something very important was about to happen in the silence surrounding the peoples of the earth, although it was hard to discern it among all the other, more conspicuous things. Men were aware that they possessed a countenance of their own, and now even those who had never mattered before were aware of it.

"Shall we get started?" he said to Lampinen, and took hold of the handcart himself.

Lampinen's sense of what was living and tender did not fail him. Going forward, he broke off the brightest and frailest sprig of the birch tree and tucked it in among the rags on the girl's breast, like a friendly banner of life.

Four: At the Pier

Myyriäinen was not sure that the girl did not hear every word Lampinen said.

He could not see her face as he went along, but he knew that her eyes were wide open and that she was not asleep. She had not slept the whole time. She had not closed her eyes since she had returned to consciousness. She stared out into the air with an oddly stiff and unblinking gaze, and one did not know if she could notice things or if her soul took recourse to its last stores of strength for the single purpose of keeping her burning eyes from falling shut.

Myyriäinen was glad he could not see her eyes. Lampinen was boasting about his erotic achievements. He became absorbed by the intimate details of intercourse, and could not get his fill of describing Palaga's lush charms. He was immeasurably proud of having such a wife. He spat to the right and the left as he walked, taking long and powerful steps to show what a remarkable fellow he was, although he was short of stature and quite a mild kind of person in other respects.

"Palaga won't put up with any scamping in these matters, you see," he chuckled delightedly. "Somebody else would probably be a little careful now and then, because the cottage is full of children, but she won't stand for it. She wants to have hers, and there's nothing that can be done about it."

Myyriäinen thought of the depths of obscure indignation and too-great knowledge which must have lain underneath little Sanni's womanly gaze. For her, Palaga's constant pregnancies meant that her serfdom never came to an end, and that she could never go to school like other girls and boys. How cunningly she must have examined her mother, teaching herself to discover the first repulsive signs of pregnancy in this tireless bearer of children.

Such considerations did not bother Lampinen. He did not see them, they simply did not exist for him. He had put them aside once and for all, like everything else which was not the way it should be in his life. Things were the way they were because God wanted to have them that way, and Iivana Lampinen was a poor sinful creature. Otherwise, he was not a callous man, and he was as proud of his children as if he had made each and every one of them with his own hands. He even treated little Sanni with a tender care which was all the more heart-warming because it was completely simple and sincere. Myyriäinen could not get enough of the little encounters which took place between father and daughter during the journey. Lampinen entertained the girl with small talk while she urinated, and then he let her rest for a while against his chest, touching his lips quite lightly on her cheek, so that their life-spirits might commune with one another. It was like looking at a pious legend. The bond between the two had a sensual intensity and spiritual absorption which contrasted in a strange way to the obvious casualness they otherwise demonstrated in their relationship. There was a great deal about them which captivated Myyriäinen precisely because it was so incalculable and self-contradictory and seemed not at all to function in the way one expected. The filth and the smell inside the girl's rags revolted him as a sign of incomprehensible indolence and thoughtlessness, but in the next moment he was deeply touched by the refined sensitivity of Lampinen's movements as he raised the girl up and supported her head against his hand; it was as though his hand had never had to do with anything save delicate and fragile things. Only Lampinen, too, by means of his cheerful face and the twinkle in his eyes, could bring forth a smile on the girl's stiffened features, and yet at bottom she had much more trust in the stranger than in Lampinen, who was her own father.

Myyriäinen decided that the girl would never have come to believe in a miracle if she had not had the sort of father she did, and if she had not imbibed a feeling with her very mother's milk that one could not be sure of anything and could not know what this or that event would entail. Observing Lampinen and his general manner of life, one was simply forced to give up preconceived opinions, and to prepare for the unforeseen. The part of Lampinen that was so infinitely undependable and ran along by chance was simultaneously that side of his character which was vital and full of imagination, and which imparted itself to others as a kind of stimulant. This thought filled Myyriäinen with a sense of cheerful recklessness, as if he had unexpectedly come into possession of a fortune. Secret reservoirs existed, despite everything, and men were perhaps not as destitute, after all, as one sometimes tended to think.

He was surprised that he had not grasped the charm of Lampinen's chatter—a little capricious and disconnected, but always picturesque and shrewd—from the very beginning. He had let it go past his ear the way he did when he wanted to pursue his own thoughts in peace. But once he had discovered its melody, he did not want to lose a single word. It was not just because Lampinen entertained him with unvarnished depictions of his marital and domestic life and, using comical turns of phrase and lightning-quick notions and drastic comparisons, described both the life and the general philosophy of the village where he lived, an Orthodox village, small and backward, a sort of last fortress of old-fashionedness in an otherwise Lutheran parish which was exemplary in every respect. More than anything else, it was the spirit of what Lampinen said that won his heart. It was his trustfulness, his captivating frankness and lack of suspicion toward a stranger, which made an impression on the melancholy Myyriäinen. Like the elusive melody in an unpretentious little folksong, this spirit was woven through the whole vivid composition of whims and gaudily painted pictures which Lampinen conjured up on the spot from his inexhaustible supply of observations and wisdom.

Later on, when Myyriäinen got to know the people in our village and the curious recluses who had found sanctuary there, it was this same spirit which captured his heart.

Reaching the top of the last ridge, he caught sight of the lake. He had sensed its nearness for a good while. Even though the waters of the great lake were not salt like those of the sea, they were strong enough to fill the air which passed through the pines with a special aroma, and although there was no breeze in particular, the sighing of the forest took on a kind of heavy roar it had not had before. The sight of the lake made an overwhelming impression on Myyriäinen. It seemed to him that these waters were unlike any others he had seen. Perhaps it was because he knew how dangerous the lake was, for a freak of its capricious spirit could cost even experienced sailors their lives; perhaps, too, because he thought of the secluded spiritual life which the mighty well-spring had protected and preserved, and of the pious hermits who century after century had gazed at the waters in silent meditation. This restless lake lay quite still now in the shine of the evening sun, and not a sound was heard over the endless surface, which seemed to tremble, echoing the final notes of the hymn of the Mother of God.

How quiet and removed from time the atmosphere of the lonely landing was, with the fog-gray boards and the graying bark-roof of the ramshackle shed! In the middle of the space before the shed a lone wagon stood sleeping. The rapt serenity which lay upon the scene made one think that these things had long ago ceased to hear the tolling strokes of time. The monks' motorboat, painted blue, lay lost in slumber, and was very like some timeless bird which had settled down here to rest. The eternal sentries looked out with their dark faces over a forgotten land.

Myyriäinen shoved Sanni's cart up to the water's edge so that she would feel herself encompassed by the spirit of the lake. Then he laid himself down at full length on the sand, stretching his stiffened legs. The sand, baked in the sun, exuded warmth; he sank into it as if into a nest, listening to the water which splashed gently against the stones on the shore. Life closed around him, familiar and secure. A light evening breeze arose and passed across his face and his hair like a caress. Lampinen hovered around him on his cat-feet; the sweetish, pungent smell from his stubby pipe spread through the air. Myyriäinen lay with his eyes closed, pretending that he slept. Lampinen felt a mighty desire to talk, but if there was any human right which he regarded as inviolable, it was the right to sleep, when one wished and where one wished, and just as long as one wanted to. Resigned to his fate, he settled down beside his comrade; he pulled his knees up under his chin and turned his thin, tanned Indian's face, seamed with a thousand meaningful wrinkles, toward the water and the evening sun. Myyriäinen could hear the faint thump as Lampinen sat down, and a smile passed over his face.

He felt that he and the man who sat there, thinking to himself, somehow belonged together. He shared something with him, a kind of brotherhood. The two of them partook equally of this little pilgrimage and the small and intimate tasks to which it gave rise. And they had a great deal else in common too, the whole Lampinen family and that funny village of theirs, somewhere in the distance, and all those good saints who were not taken so terribly seriously but whom one liked to have around just the same. After a single day of being together with Lampinen, he felt like a member of the family. He thought that he in fact knew all of them, not just Lampinen himself and little Sanni, but the seven other children too, all the way down to the newborn infant which had not even been baptized yet, and Palaga, rosy-cheeked and lush, the mother, whom he pictured for himself as a kind of rustic goddess of fertility. He was also familiar with Natalia Ivanovna, the teacher of religion, who would not leave Lampinen in peace because Sanni did not get to go to school, and the one-eyed postman, Tommi, the village oracle, and the incomparable Assendorff, and the frightful, sharp-nosed old witch-woman Olsbom, at whose place Assendorff lived, and of course he was also acquainted with Matvej Olkkonen, the fat and genial merchant, who knew everything and was the village's Don Juan. He saw them before him in clear colors, as one sees the pictures in a storybook, and he had a vivid impression that all these people were actually children, big, clumsy, good-natured children who had built a village of their own somewhere in a quiet corner.

This was why he felt such a longing to join them. He thought that if an oasis where living waters rippled still existed anywhere in the world, then it must be there, where these people lived in the midst of their saints and their dead as if nothing had happened which could cut them off from the light of heaven. A community must exist there, for there dwelt a childlike spirit. Even if the old-fashioned religion had grown weak in the people's conscious mind, it had still protected and preserved their emotions and the most sensitive organs of their souls from the desolation which too much loneliness can cause.

He was filled with gratitude toward the little pilgrim company of two which had met him on his journey and had made him one of them.

While he lay listening to the wind's gentle sighing and the water's murmur, he thought he detected something like a rush of lament within the air. It seemed to be a cry of woe from tormented hearts, an ancient lament which rang beneath the vaults of the centuries and reverberated in this place, where endless trains of pilgrims had gone past, bearing their immeasurable cares. Shadows pressed around him, then glided away in the twilight of the ages; he thought that even though the pilgrims had vanished, their cares had stayed behind on this lonely shore. A thousand years had vanished like a day, and mankind was still bent beneath the burden of its cross, and could not save itself from evil, nor even send the weakest beam of light into the night of death.

Altogether confused, he sat up; he did not know where he was. Sometimes, when he had been lost in thoughts, it was impossible for him to find his way back to reality at once. He had heard a noise which awakened him from his dreams. His glance fell on the old jetty, gray as the fog, and the blue boat beside it. He looked at it as if he had never seen it before, and it occurred to him that the soul perhaps descended down from just such a landing into Charon's boat on the black river.

As though by magic, the shore was filled with life and movement. The monks and their followers arrived with a tremendous hullaballoo. In the Carelian way, the peasants drove as fast as they could until they stopped; the handsome horses were brought up with a jerk, snorting and panting in their impatience and overexcitement. The drivers threw down their reins carelessly, as if they wanted to show how complete their control over their horses was. They were all in high spirits: they took out bundles and greasy packages, they yelled, they ran back and forth, they gesticulated and chattered. An unmistakable atmosphere of worldly good-humoredness and geniality lay upon the group; the good food and the successful business deals could be smelled from far away. The hosts had not been sparing with refreshments, and the monks on their side had partaken enthusiastically of the gifts of God. The smell, affirming life by its very existence, tickled Myyriäinen's nose like the odor of fresh-baked bread. He felt immensely cheerful himself. Whatever objection could be made to these monks, they did not have the air of being some fading remnant from the past. Their heavy bodies and bearded faces gave the impression of a peasant's solid vitality. One could easily see that physical labor was their pious exercise and that in their reverence they had retained their contact with the earth. A childlike simplicity and gladness shone out of their clear eyes, and a winning benevolence characterized their whole manner.

Iivana Lampinen was completely at home here. Jumping up quickly, he mixed into the crowd in order to take part in everything that occurred. He went from one person to the next, telling them with an important expression that he was on the way to the Mother of God in search of a cure for his sick child. The short, thickset worker-monks listened to him with touching earnestness, although most of them did not understand a word of what he said. In their long kaftans and heavy oiled-leather boots, they darted back and forth between the carts and the boat as nimbly as weasles; but as soon as they discovered that a sick child lay on the handcart and that succor was being sought from the Madonna, they all gathered around the girl, chattering like magpies. Standing with their heads on one side, they looked at her with expressions of sympathy and wonderment in their bright and guileless eyes.

The monks rejoiced in their hearts at the arrival of the little band of pilgrims. It had been a long time since the song of pilgrim-flocks had resounded beneath the vaults of their cloister. Gone were those rich and mighty folk who once had knelt in the cloister's church, gone too the poor people, the little people who had come in unending streams out of the vastnesses of holy Russia. Now and then, of course, some secretly burdened soul came to pray beside the silver sarcophagus and to light his candle before the wonder-working icon; now and then a little flock came from the district's scattered congregations in order to see the sights of the venerable place and to perform its divine service there; but for the most part the mighty cloister church stood empty. Within her covering of silver and precious stones, weakly illuminated by the prayer-lamp's glow, the Virgin Mother awaited those believing hearts which knew no aid save recourse to her gentle intercession.

When the monks had returned to their labor, Myyriäinen went up to Sanni. She lay as she had before, her eyes wide open and staring, and one cheek was red as fire. There was something terrible about her face now. He could not stand to look at her, knowing how she must suffer. He turned his glance away. Then he caught sight of the priest-monk, who was walking in their direction. The monk had a solemn, measured tread which made one immediately set him apart from the other monks. He stopped still for a moment, gazing at the girl. Then he raised three fingers, blessed her, and included her in his prayer. He grew noticeably paler when he was absorbed in his devotions, and, as at their first meeting, Myyriäinen had the same overwhelming sensation of a force which emanated from the monk. Even before he had finished his prayer and blessed her once again, with movements which were simple, yet somehow strong and intense, the girl lay submerged in sleep.

That man had the power to bless.

He gave Myyriäinen a friendly glance in passing and walked on with the same stately tread as before. Shortly thereafter he took part in the cheerful hubbub at the water's edge, to all appearances completely calm and natural in his manner. From one side, Myyriäinen stood watching it all as if in a dream.

He could not free himself from the impression that he had been here before, a long time ago, perhaps in some other existence. These solemn scenes of parting, these kisses, these movements of the hands—it seemed as though he groped through his all too limited memory for motifs from Christianity's first days and from Greece and the Orient, it seemed as though he saw them preserved here by some mysterious process, in the soft earth of the Finnish folksong. He easily recognized these peasants and merchants, they were blood of his blood, lively, voluble, with the genuine Carelian glint in their eye, yet there was something in their expressive gestures and in the abrupt transitions from earnestness to naive hilarity which appeared foreign to him. A whole world of strange traditions and symbols lay behind their hearts' most intimate expressions. A more ancient and gentler faith had exercised its influence upon their character, their vital sense had received another color and another tone, a melody from the beginning of time, unfathomable and yet so simple that one could have grasped it if one had been a child.

And they seemed to shy away from the final departure,

forgetting it, as it were, for moments on end, as is the practice of children and old people. There was always something that was missing or something that was wrong or whatever else could provide an excuse for delay. They looked at one another, they cast their glances out over the waters. They asked questions without getting answers, they waited without knowing what they were waiting for. Obviously, no one wanted to take the trouble to find out what it was. They were satisfied anyway. They were alive. They had more time than anything else. In short, they were immortal. Myyriäinen was struck by the rightness of their thought. After all, time simply glided out of man's hands, and the more he hurried, the more inexorably and swiftly it slipped away. Then why should a man fetter his existence to time? He should make himself independent of it. That is what children did, that is what old people did, and that is what these people did too. They were at home in existence as in their father's house. No matter what they undertook, there was nothing which had to be done in a rush. Life stayed with them in any case.

"Whoever does not receive the kingdom of God as a child does, will never enter into it," Myyriäinen thought as he stood looking at them.

Finally the neglectful leader of the monks came running down the bank to the shore, his hat askew and the folds of his habit fluttering around his legs, the very picture of the most obliging sort of officiousness. There was a new saying of farewells, there were new blessings and embraces and final admonitions. Myyriäinen carefully took Sanni in his arms, and Lampinen put her little cart beside the peaceful old wagon, whose purpose here no one knew. All of a sudden there was a great rush, and people crowded onto the narrow jetty, cheerfully shoving themselves forward in order to get some relief from the excitement which a journey over the water always causes in the world's children, no matter who they are. A hum like a beehive's arose from the overloaded boat, the motor spluttered and whined, but the girl slept on.

During the trip the monks grew grave and silent. No one said a word. They sat quietly and solemnly, their rough laborer's hands in their laps, and looked straight ahead, as if they did not want to allow their bright eyes to get lost somewhere on the horizon. Even Lampinen seemed to be gripped by the seriousness of the occasion and did not make a sound. The lake's expanse lay smooth as a mirror in the sunset, and on the horizon the cloister's flaming cupola rose up like a vision from the past.

In the light haze of gold above the waters, the memory of Him Who had rebuked the waves and the wind upon the Lake of Gennesaret shone like a figure in a dream.

Five: The Miracle

During the passage Myyriäinen had been seized by the demon of fear.

Sanni's peaceful sleep had turned into a heavy, agonized unconsciousness. Gurgling sounds pressed forth from her throat, and spasms of twitching ran through her body. Her bluish face changed with each moment that passed, assuming more and more that fearful aspect a face gets when death has made its last brutal incision into the living tissues. "We'll get there too late, we'll get there too late," said the hammering in Myyriäinen's brain. He was overwhelmed by a sense of life's impotence. He felt tired unto death. Everything that had been elevating and mystically transcendent in the mood which lately had filled him disappeared, and he had a nauseating sensation of corruption and fatigue. Something heavy spread itself over his soul. All the accreted mortal fear of the age seemed to press down upon his breast. Dark faces with malignant expressions rose up from his nocturnal dreams, dreams about dead men he did not know, and the earth groaned beneath the weight of corpses which lay piled upon it. His thoughts circled unceasingly around a single and terrible word, and that word was corpse. He tried with all his might to drive the thought away, but it came back again and again, biting itself fast into his consciousness. There was something in the word itself which he did not wish to think to an end, something evil and repulsive which it was not fitting for him to think to an end. A picture which he had seen somewhere in a newspaper came to the surface of his memory, a picture of some children, mutilated and burned, on a street in Shanghai, and it seemed as though only this single picture was needed to open the gate of the Kingdom of the Dead within him. One image after another came forward with terrifying clarity, maimed, tortured, fear-driven figures, as they had accumulated on the bottom of his consciousness during the years of suffering. The phantoms pointed at the small charred corpses in Shanghai with hideous delight, and he heard a voice which said: "Suffer the little children to come unto me, and forbid them not; for to such belongeth the Kingdom of God."

He imagined that an abyss opened before him, and that he could not keep from throwing himself into it with a cry.

As the boat slowly pulled alongside the cloister's jetty, a remarkable calm descended upon him. Bending down over little Sanni, he saw that her spirit had not yet fled. The death struggle continued as before, but he watched it without fear. As soon as he set foot on the cloister's island, he knew that a miracle would take place. As though enclosed within an invisible magnetic field, he ascended the hill with the dying child in his arms. He paid no attention to what was happening around him and seemed scarcely conscious of his companions' existence. He moved with great lightness, without being sensible of his own body, like a pilgrim who has been under way for a long time and who finally feels the holy earth beneath his feet. He did not turn around a single time to admire the unique beauty of the place to which he so unexpectedly had come. He did not see the lake's magical play in the sunset nor the roses' luxuriant glow against the stern white walls. The sentimental values which the cloister as a form of life can offer to the chance visitor did not exist for him. He had business with the Mother of God, and he was aware of nothing else.

Iivana Lampinen trudged along at his side, the last feeble heir to a spiritual empire which counted Jesus Christ as its founder. Zealous and not a little proud, he kept getting underfoot; he pulled at his comrade's arm, pointing at first one thing and then another with the expression of a child who wants to show his treasures to an outsider. Now that he had actually arrived, he was seized by the atmosphere of the holy place, entering into a state of euphoria and mild intoxication which was not so very different from the pious ecstasy which had gripped the pilgrims of former days upon their first sight of the wonder-working Madonna's sanctuary. Myyriäinen was not aware of Lampinen's overtures and comprehended his chatter no more than he did the sound of the lake's waters. His strange inaccessibility made Lampinen turn rather thoughtful. Was it perhaps a holy man whom he had come upon by accident? Or what else could it be that had wrought such a change in his friend?

The fact that his comrade's condition, so much like a sleepwalker's, made an impression on Iivana Lampinen was not surprising. He had no experience of the enormous tensions that are released within the soul when it suddenly enters into contact with the invisible world after a profound absence. For all his worldliness and naive superficiality, he himself lived within the invisible realm as in the very air he breathed, like a child who is so absorbed by a game that he thinks of nothing save the vicarious meaning the game has given the objects with which he plays. It was natural for him to communicate with the invisible world, just as natural as it was to lift up his soul into a union with that of some other human being. Indeed, to his eyes temporal authority was much more mystic and distant than were the silent protectors with whom he had been familiar since his childhood.

As a matter of fact, going to one side of the church steps in order to relieve himself before entering the sanctuary, he cast a shy sidelong glance at his stern and silent comrade. But above the portal of the church there stood an icon which he knew well and loved, and this sight gave him a feeling of security as he did his business. He crossed himself, in a friendly but somewhat hurried manner, before the blessed being which gazed down upon him through the image's eyes, and hastened to follow Myyriäinen into the temple.

Except for a single suppliant beside the high altar, the great cloister church was empty. With half-closed eyelids, Myyriäinen went straight across the floor and up to the Madonna. He moved with a calm surety as though he knew the place well. Lampinen hurried forward in his self-important way in order to awaken the girl. Gliding out like a shadow from somewhere or other, the priest-monk stopped him. "The Holy Mother of God will rouse her when the time has come," he said in a low voice, and then disappeared.

Holding the girl in his arms, Myyriäinen stood unmoving before the miraculous icon. Lampinen knelt by his side. He mumbled his prayers briskly, sighed heavily a couple of times, crossed himself, and made such a deep bow that his forehead touched the floor. Every now and then he looked up with his clear eyes at God's Mother and at the two small candles he had lit before her image, one for himself and one for his sick child. In the flickering candles' beam, the jewels of her setting glittered with a living light that could mean many things. An atmosphere of intense expectation formed around the little group. Pulses pounded, frail blood vessels contracted, and nerves trembled at an unfamiliar touch. The deepening silence around the Madonna was broken only by choked, guttural sounds and feeble death rattles. Myyriäinen's heart was calm. Neither unrest nor hesitation plagued him. He stood where he should stand, that was all. A child of man would have her fate confirmed and sealed, once and for all, as it is proper for one who belongs to an order of things not governed by chance. He did not notice time's passage. He did not know whether hours or minutes went by. Lampinen had gone away and come back and disappeared again, but he had no awareness of it. The candles had flared up one last time and gone out. He did not notice. He had his eyes fixed unswervingly upon the magnificent icon. And the more he looked at it, the more living the Madonna's mild and darkened face became. It seemed to float forth from the heavy setting—the setting whose splendor human hands had assembled—dissolving into a transcendent expression of care which pierced straight into his heart.

The Child Jesus on the Madonna's arm toyed with two small heavenly doves.

Did her lips move, or was it only a trick of his imagination? A faint tremble passed through the body of the dying child. Myyriäinen looked around, as if involuntarily seeking support from someone else. There was no one in the church. He was alone with what would happen. The girl uttered a sound of lament. Her body contracted, then raised itself, as in the birth pangs of death, and her face froze in an expression of brutal pain. Myyriäinen did not take his eyes from it. "I shall see it, I shall not turn my glance away," he said to himself. His heart was calm. He knew that this was not the end. But his hands which bore the little bundle trembled with exhaustion and terror.

Suddenly her features were made smooth, as if by a gentle hand, and the strain in the tormented body gave way. Her breast lifted itself once or twice, she let a gentle sigh escape, and then there came that great stillness which portends life's extinction. A frozen calm descended upon the face.

"Her heart has stopped beating," Myyriäinen thought. "Sanni has gone without regaining consciousness."

All of a sudden, the bundle grew terribly heavy in his arms. A feeling of desolation, of loneliness, came upon him. Was there nothing more? Little Sanni was gone, like the myriads of other dead, and that was all. God the Father had forgotten a sparrow. He turned his eyes away. He wished to see her face no longer. He thought that it must have changed. Something strange and terrible must have entered into it. He was seized by sympathy for poor little Sanni, who was dead. He remembered the words so well which she had spoken when she still existed, and how with her officiousness she had tried to drive away the shadow which had descended upon her path: "—and so they say that somebody's dead and stuff him into the ground." He felt sorry for everyone who was dead. How homeless they were, cast out into a fathomless darkness where not a single friend could follow them. And he would also die and be left in loneliness without a single friend. He stood trembling before the source of his own feeling of isolation; he saw how lonely all men in fact were, and why they were so lonely and could not be otherwise, however much they tried to hide it from themselves.

In his distress, he thought that since Sanni was dead he would not go along with Lampinen as he had agreed. What reason did he have for visiting the strange village?

He was about to leave, yet he could not help casting a last glance upon her face. There he saw that something like a light cloud, bearing life's color, lay upon it. As he watched, she opened her eyes. They were clearer than he had ever seen them before, illuminated through and through by the uncompromising light of consciousness. Without knowing what he did, he moved a step nearer to the icon and raised up the dying girl as high as the Child Jesus and the small white doves of the image. A sweet and half-surprised smile glided over her face, and her hand made a weak movement, as though to seize life's fading visions. With a clear but somewhat unfamiliar voice she spoke the words: "Sanni Maria Lampinen, Iivana's daughter," as her name was written in the church register. There was a strange echo in the old arches, as if God the Father Himself, mumbling, had repeated this mortal being's name. For a moment it filled the spaces of the temple, mirroring itself with a dusky golden shine in the ornaments of the iconostasis. Angelic choirs repeated it through the eons of time.

When Sanni had fulfilled the demand of her spirit, raising herself up to the dignity of those who have been given names, she collapsed in her exhaustion and died. On her countenance was an expression of finality and perfect peace which words cannot express; only a faint trace of froth around her lips bore witness to the last defense she had made of her life.

He contemplated the expression on Sanni's dead face. He would have liked to take it with him, to devote the remainder of his life to its study. He guessed that he could never be finished with it. It was consummate. Here, a child of man had finally found itself. It was a miracle: the greatest of all the earth's miracles had taken place before his eyes, and he realized that whosoever could be touched by this miracle would be freed from his chains.

What was this enigmatic perfection's source? Was it not this same perfection which rendered the work of a human hand immortal? He thought of the poor name which the dying child had uttered in the knowledge that it was the most important component of her life, and the only one to which God's Mother would pay attention, and he was struck by the thought that the name had been lifted up to the same rank and dignity as those of the immortal masters. How mysterious is the knowledge that one possesses a name—a name confers a countenance upon a human being, and this countenance is as perfect in the least of men as in the mightiest; one must merely learn to tell it apart, refusing to be led astray by whatever else one sees.

He felt the need to talk with his dead friend, and to come close to her, as close as it was possible for a living being to come to a dead one. He wished to feel that the contact between them had not been broken. He thought he would put his cheek against her cheek and speak softly to her, as one speaks to the flowers and trees which have no voice. But a curious shyness held him back. The dead girl rested like a Sleeping Beauty within her enchanted castle, and he did not know what he must say to approach her. He felt so poor with his clumsy words and his memory which went no further than to his own childhood. He imagined that she knew so much more about life than he himself could remember. She knew more than any living being about all the dead people and the dead trees and the ancient stones which lay concealed in the earth. She knew more than any living being about all those mute things which lay concealed within the earth and within the breast of men, all that which had never achieved expression or consciousness, and which had existed since the dawn of time. He remembered the old and hallowed words: "From dust you have come, and to dust you shall return," and he felt that they contained another import than that of darkness and decay. A memory of an obscure connection with the dead stirred in the depths of his soul, and it seemed as though his own existence suddenly became only a thin membrane which separated him from the maternal womb where all that is living and all that is dead repose in a mute and indissoluble communion.

He bent down and gave little Sanni a kiss.

And he got the feeling that the dead girl wished to tell him something. The deep serenity on her face seemed to form itself into a word, a great and soft and single word, which contained all other words within itself and gave them meaning. He felt that he was the one who was mute, that it was the dead girl who spoke. She talked unchangingly and serenely about something which he could not grasp, although he knew all the while what it was, about something which he perhaps had seen in his distracted dreams, or heard in a moment of secret inspiration, and he knew that if he could remember it, then he would understand what she said and receive such joy from her as he could never get from any living being.

"We can say she's really happy now. May God be merciful to her little soul."

Lampinen had entered unnoticed; he stood looking at his dead child. He seemed quite satisfied. There were no signs that the event had grieved him deeply in any way. He knelt down with utmost serenity, crossed himself before the Most Holy Madonna, and spoke a prayer for the soul of the departed. When he got up, an expression of apprehensiveness, of worry, entered his face. He rubbed his nose reflectively, wondering what Palaga was going to say about this useless journey now. The creature could have died at home just as well as in this cloister, she'd say, and Lampinen would not have needed to loaf away three days on the journey's account.

"It will be a first-class funeral just the same," he said a little hesitatingly. And after a while, in order to provide a further justification: "And you can't help thinking that she'll sleep with a lighter heart now."

Myyriäinen turned little Sanni over to Lampinen and his quiet speculations; then he left the temple.

As he opened the door of the dark church, a blinding flame burst upon him. The short summer night was at an end, and the sun had risen. He turned his grayish face toward the sun's blessed light as though astounded. A thrill of joy ran through him, and with all his being, with his skin and with his limbs, he felt the incomprehensible sweetness of existence.

Half dazed, like someone surprised by an unknown joy, he started to walk out into the moorland which began behind the cloister, stretching toward the island's interior. His step was unsure, he stumbled over tussocks and the roots of trees. A fresh wind blew in from the lake, and the air above the moor's harsh landscape was filled with strong odors of forest and earth and water. He went through old gates, past garden plots and meadowlands, and at last entered the forest. The terrain grew rougher and gloomier, great moss-covered boulders were piled one upon the other, and dark spruces stood in impenetrable and menacing groves in the dank hollows between the stretches of rock. There were neither paths nor trails here. At times he had to creep along on his hands and knees, at times he was stopped by sudden precipices. As he gazed down into the magic depths, he had an intense sensation of joy. This nature's inaccessibility, the fact that it could not be tamed, lured him onward like some dark fate, and he let his soul have its fill of the wild ravines' melancholy. He often stood for a long time, leaning against a stone and gazing down into the glittering green of the mossy gloom beneath the trees. What spirits might have their abode here? What gods waited beneath the rocks for their resurrection? The primeval forest brooded over its secrets only a short distance from the Cross of Christ, and no one could know when lichen and moss would conquer the frail symbols of man, erasing the traces of his searching and formative spirit.

He was so lost in his thoughts that he did not notice the hermit's hut before he was directly upon it. It was not very different from the earth. It was as gray as the stone against which it leaned, and a scrubby old spruce sheltered it with its branches. A short distance from it, on a knoll in the open, there stood a little chapel, as grizzled and tumble-down as the cabin itself. There was something pathetic about the lonely settlement; it seemed defenseless against the powers which reigned here. He wondered to himself if the last hermit lay buried beneath the knoll. Soon, like the hermit, the cross on the church would rot in the woods. He clambered up onto the boulder beside the hut, seating himself there as if to observe the decline and fall. Then a monotonous and rhythmic sound reached his ear, a sound which could only be produced by a human being. It came from the chapel and in the midst of this wilderness moved him in a strange way. He listened enchanted to the rising and falling progressions of the ritual hymn, and he realized that a hermit still dwelt here and that he was just now performing his matutinal devotions in the chapel's closed chamber. It was a mysterious office in this lonely place.

The being who finally appeared was curious indeed: a misshapen cripple who could move only with great difficulty, in an endless and disgusting series of twists and jerks. His hair was long and straggling, and his face, sickly pale, was almost covered over with his beard and with dirt. The first glimpse of this wretched and neglected hermit's hut of a body was repulsive, and Myyriäinen had cause to think of what he had heard about the darker aspects of life among the Orthodox monks. But as soon as the monk had come forward to him, greeting him with a blessing and a friendly glance from his clear blue eyes, the unpleasant impression disappeared. He inspired trust. From the first moment on, something about him made one feel that nothing need to be kept secret from him, that he understood everything, that he wished one well. "He has a right to be called Father," Myyriäinen thought. The hermit did not seem to be at all surprised or in any way troubled by the unexpected visit. Going into the cabin, he returned with a piece of coarse black bread in his hand. He broke the bread, blessed it, and, jerking and nodding involuntarily, handed half of it to his guest. Myyriäinen reverently took the sweet-smelling bread, with its dark shine, from the hermit's trembling hand. It was not a piece of ordinary bread with which to fill his stomach. It was like a living being, a product of sun and earth and rain, an uncommon gift of nature. The hermit ate his part of the bread with a pious and concentrated repose, as if he were receiving a sacrament. "One should always eat that way," Myyriäinen thought to himself.

When the monk had finished eating, he broke the silence.

"My son," he said. "Have you noticed that the Angel of Death has returned to the earth? His shadow has been visible for two years now."

Myyriäinen looked at the hermit in surprise; it was as though the monk had read his most secret thoughts, and knew the springs of fear that rose within him.

"Every day at the morning mass I pray for those who fell in the World War," the hermit continued. "This is my mission in the world of the spirit. And when one consorts with the dead, one gets to know a great deal. Only this morning, at the rising of the sun, when I was about to recite my prayers, I heard a mighty roar which overwhelmed my soul and made me mute. I should have thought that my God had abandoned me, if I had not known that it was the Angel of Death, spreading out his wings."

He became lost in contemplation, and Myyriäinen did not dare to disturb him with a single question. He realized that, in his way, the hermit had knowledge of what was going on in the world; perhaps he had a clearer and broader view than those who were in its midst, aware of nothing other than their own obscure anxiety.

In a while the hermit began to tell modestly and simply of his own life. He had taken part in the World War himself, somewhere in the Carpathians. He was young then, not much more than a boy. Before the first year was over, the war had spat him out again, a human wreck. He found life and the men who lived it so loathsome that he felt he could overcome his disgust only in the seclusion of the cloister. He wished to find the most lonely place of all, and God prepared a refuge for him here. Even during his existence as a monk he had gone through many temptations. But the rigorous asceticism of his life, his prayers, and an utter submission to the will of the cloister's eldest member had helped him to win peace. And when God in His mercy had let him reach the highest stage of the ascetic, a hermit's life, he had finally got to taste the indescribable spiritual joy which complete renunciation can bestow.

"And now I also know more than I knew before about the task the Angel of Death has had placed before him. When he returns to the earth and spreads out his wings, a storm will go through the hearts of men. The spiritual man will loose himself from the straits of his living death, and be liberated unto a true life of joy."

He suddenly directed a piercing glance at the stranger.

"You shall not be afraid, my son," he said with a strong and sonorous tone altogether unlike his usual trembling voice. "Before you close your eyes, you will see how the whited sepulchres are opened, and how the living dead are resurrected to a new life. The people of the earth will cry: Praised be the Lord, Hallelujah!"

He said nothing more, but got up from his place and entered his hut, as if he had already forgotten that he had just been speaking with someone.

Myyriäinen remained sitting there, absorbed in his reflections. Somehow, Sanni's death and the great and gentle word she had wanted to say to him and the terror he had himself endured were interwoven with what the monk had said, and he got the feeling that not only he but all men, the whole of humanity, were about to be transformed by the radiance of a mystery, just as the blood in the holy chalice was transformed, becoming alive.

He arose in order to return to his friends.

Six: The Arrival

Our village can seem insignificant and of little importance, lying secluded as it does in an out-of-the-way corner of the parish, squeezed in between the river and the stony hills, poor and gray and run-down, and hidden besides in a spiritual sense from the eyes of the world on account of its Orthodox faith and its old-fashioned customs; but its people are more cheerful than in most other places, and nowhere in the world is the stranger as well received as here. He needs merely to put his foot on the village path—bumpy and half grown over, meandering gracefully alongside sparse pastures and around little hills—in order to feel that it is a beginning of the road to serenity and truth. The fresh, damp air from the river and from the gum alders down in the hollow immediately meets the wanderer; and if he chances upon someone from the village, some wily old man, or a flock of inquisitive children or a brown-eyed woman with her skirts tucked up and a child on her arm, he will experience—perhaps for the first time in his life—the fascination of pleasing his fellow men, of giving them delight by his mere existence. It is this very circumstance which makes a stranger feel so extremely happy in our village, and which has vouchsafed so many souls—generous ones, to be sure, but grown thorny from life's wounds—a sanctuary and a refuge from the harassments of fate.

Here, hospitality is not just a virtue but an inherent necessity which even the poorest and most wretched person allows himself to satisfy. It's wonderful to have strangers around, they feel, and they value nothing more highly than a quiet exchange of thoughts. An animal-lover would perhaps have some criticisms to make of the people here, for the horses are treated so badly that it's a shame, and God alone knows how the cats and dogs with which the village teems get their share of food. But our village is a paradise for someone who loves human beings. No matter whether he is bad or good, poor or rich, a person is treated not only with equanimity but with genuine affection. Even a beggar can feel like a man who has something of value stored away inside him, even though he doesn't have very much in his bag. The rather sly curiosity and inclination to gossip one can notice here is basically of a benevolent nature; it conceals a spiritual tolerance and a joy at human nature—human nature taken just the way it is—that beams with an invigorating force on every stranger who, for whatever reason, happens to find his way here.

The incomparable Assendorff, for example, who was engaged in a feud with God and the whole world, and who could no longer find a single person willing to receive him and his tattered dragoon's cape beneath his roof; where could so pugnacious a soul have found a sanctuary, if the peasants here had not taken an interest in him, letting him fish in their waters, letting him fool along with one thing and another in their forests? They merely laughed at the pickles he got himself into and if the situation seemed to be taking a really serious turn, they made the sign of the cross and said: "God be merciful to his soul." Poor unhappy Schwancken was a similar case: he had run away from his elegant father and his crazy mother, and lived like an animal in the woods, sleeping in crevices in the rocks and eating roots and berries. No doubt he would have hanged himself from a tree long ago if the young owner of Vornikka farm, himself a little of a hermit, had not caught him in his pea-patch and made a human being out of him again. What did the farmer actually do on that occasion? He just sat looking at Schwancken from his hiding place, and after he had watched for a while, he discovered that it was an unfortunate man on whom he gazed. He crept up quietly and grabbed the thief by the neck. Schwancken defended himself furiously, but could not pull loose. When he realized that he was caught, he curled up between the pea vines and lay there quite still. Then the young farmer sat down beside him, as if nothing at all had happened and as if the place was the most natural one in the world for a conversation, and began to talk calmly and reasonably, as was his custom. He talked about what concerned him most and what he had read about in all the books he owned, about a way of life in harmony with nature, about horticulture, and about the destiny of mankind. The despairing Schwancken lay there listening to him, just as the ground lies listening to the gentle rain in springtime. They left the pea-patch as friends for life, and now there is nothing in seven parishes like the garden at Vornikka, thanks in great part to Schwancken.

And who could forget how Uncle Ungert looked when he arrived here one raw, cold October evening with his beggar's sack in his hand and his eyes like burning coals, famished and frozen in the hard wind of adversity? With his hooked nose and his hanging mustaches he looked like a Turkish bandit, and as soon as they caught sight of him, the children clung like bunches of grapes to his arms and his legs and cried out in chorus: "Tell us a story, tell us a story!" They had realized immediately that a man from the world of fairy tales and adventures stood before them in a beggar's form. And then Uncle Ungert began to tell his stories. He went into the nearest house, and the children sat down in a ring around him, and he told them about his life. It is not easy to know how much the young ones understood of all he had to say, but they listened with breathless attention, and the more strange words they heard, the more captivated they became. Their eyes grew deep and dark like the mysterious pools in the bog, and right before their bare and dirty feet a mighty and astounding world revealed itself in the twilight of the cottage. Carefully and with great gravity, as if he were handling treasures beyond price, Uncle Ungert took his memories out of the box of the past which he had carried with him for such a long time without ever opening it to look inside. He saw himself as a young cadet, storming up the stairs at the Alexejev military college, three steps at a time, as reckless and impatient as every youth is who cannot plunge into the great adventure soon enough. When the heavy oak door of the Oriental Institute in Vladivostok closed behind him, his steps were heavier and the unknown lay like a dark and alluring shadow upon his eyes. It drew him onward with an irresistible force, farther and still farther away, and wherever war burst into flame in its passage across the earth, he was to be found. Somewhere beyond Mongolia's endless steppes, in the timeless stillness beside the river Ljao-He, he arrived at the realization that his life was a pursuit of the wind. He devoted himself to highly respectable research, received the order of the Double Dragon, and the title of mandarin was bestowed upon him. That which followed, the World War, the revolution, his flight, his misery, were simply repetitions of what had gone before, but with the roles reversed: now he was not the hunter but the hunted.

"Can you go flying with the Double Dragon?" a boy asked all of a sudden, burning with suspense.

"Naturally, that's why you get to be a mandarin," Uncle Ungert answered with that unshakable earnestness which appeals to children more than any other human quality.

"Are you a real mandarin? Can you fly for us now?" the children cried, completely beside themselves from excitement.

"It can very well happen that I'll fly one day," answered Uncle Ungert in a sepulchral voice. "But I don't want to now. I'm so tired that I'll sleep for a hundred days."

The children took the explanation at face value, and this very hour they are still waiting for the hundred days to come to an end. It doesn't bother them at all to see Uncle Ungert tramp around with his bark-basket over his arm. After all, they know that the mandarin is asleep.

From that moment on Uncle Ungert was supernatural, a being of a higher sort, a half-god, the hero of whom the race of men seems to have an ineradicable need. He was never especially friendly toward the children—on the contrary, his manner was quite sullen and distant, and the very fact that he never laughed served to enhance his reputation among them. Like animals, children do not want people to laugh. His person had something of that inaccessibility and mysticism which attaches to the true magician, and this was enough to turn him into the master of unlimited possibilities, the man who can fulfill your most secret wishes with a wave of his hand, offering you a life of magnificent happenings and events which go against the order of nature. In brief: he became the mandarin of our little community. The children had never heard such a word before, but as soon as they had heard it, they grasped its incantatory and magic meaning. Thereafter, the mandarin was with them, wherever they might go, and their secret hiding places acquired a special fascination through the fact that the mandarin could conceal himself in them. He became the main character in their play-acting, and finally the children created their immortal Mandarin Game, a profoundly solemn and at the same time breakneck game which became more popular than any other in our village.

Thus it came to pass that Uncle Ungert, a man who had wandered through such a great part of our world, stopped at last in our insignificant village and became its ornament and pride. He postponed his departure from day to day, and before he knew it, years had passed by, and still he could not bring himself to leave the children. New generations of children gathered around him and listened to his tales, but he scarcely noticed the change. He saw the same expectant eyes directed toward him, and heard the same shrill voices crying "Mandarin, mandarin," and it sounded like the twitter of birds in the silent forests of his memories. And one thing is sure: as long as Uncle Ungert walks here in the flesh among these children, no one can persuade them to abandon their belief that, one fine day, he will wrap himself in the wings of the Double Dragon and fly away, big as life, with his mustaches and his hooked nose and the familiar bark-basket on his arm. Whoever refuses to believe it is no child of our village.

Actually, it was not so strange that Abel Myyriäinen, when he came trudging into our village one warm and rather sultry June evening in the company of his friend the tinker, thought to himself that he might as well stay here forever—the road leading into our village is a pretty one indeed. Of course, there was a great deal of commotion when the people in the outlying cottages caught sight of the pilgrims. The news about little Sanni's pilgrimage to the cloister had spread like wildfire, and both Natalia Ivanovna and, in particular, the Olsbom woman had expressed their views on the matter. A whole crowd of curious people, their eyes abulge, came streaming up, and Lampinen played his role as the chief figure of events with a genuine bravura. His position was truly enviable. He was not only the father of a child who had died before the eyes of the Most Holy Madonna, he was also the man who had brought along a stranger as his honored guest. The women looked at him with proper reverence, too, and no one attached much importance to the fact that Sanni had died; after all she was an odd sort of child who had not died at home in a corner by the stove. When the tinker pointed to Myyriäinen with a sweeping and chivalrous gesture of his hand and said: "This is my guest," the women made their most dignified curtsy, and the men took him stiffly by the hand, saying: "Welcome among us. It's very nice in our village this time of year."

Myyriäinen did not feel at all annoyed by the attention he received. As a matter of fact, he became quite exhilarated and chattered as freely with these people as if he had known them all his life. While Lampinen's boasting was at its height, he stood to one side and let the careless and curiously vital mood of the village street and the friendliness the people emanated penetrate to the core of his being. His first encounter with the spirit of the village told him that this was a place where a man could live, as the people say here, "lower than the grass and stiller than the water," and at this moment there was nothing he longed for more than such an intimate and hidden life. He wanted to enter some place where he would be as well concealed, as little noticed, as the seed within the earth, where people would not know what sort of person he was, and would not ask whether he remained the same or not; instead, they would let him lie quietly and be transformed.

He had been prepared for an idyl. But when, at a bend in the path, he suddenly caught sight of Lampinen's cottage on the slope, with the birches and the blooming lilac and the friendly gray hill as a shield toward the back and the potato patch and the hops which crept up the big stone beside the front stoop, he realized how insignificant and empty his own notion had been, and how much more meaningful the reality itself was. Here in this sparse forest, the house grew out of the earth in such a way as to suggest perfect and classical harmony. The ample, dark-eyed woman sat on the stoop and suckled her youngest child; the skin on her bared breast had the same dusky, sun-soaked shimmer as the patina on the house's gray gable, burned by the sun and dried by the wind. Small flaxen-haired heads and some darker ones stuck up here and there like mushrooms emerging from the earth. The earth was everything here: the cottage, the woman, the children, bread and death. Living, sun-soaked earth, the home of man.

He saw it all at once in a single glance, while he stood running his fingers over the gate which he was to open for Lampinen and little Sanni. And in the same moment he knew that the sole thing he wished for himself was to become earth of this earth, to sink into it and be united with it throughout every part of his being. "I shall bury my false tools here," he thought, "and beneath that hill over there I shall prepare a grave for the dream of my youth." As he opened the gate, he noticed that the gray woodwork within its frame had the shape of a lyre. The ornament caught his sympathy; it was an expression of Lampinen's poetic sense. In this moment, the primitive wooden lyre on the tinker's rickety gate seemed to him to be lovelier than the world's most beautiful work of art, because it had grown out of the forest's own essence in the same way as everything else here: the people, the houses, the paths, the hop garden and the potato patch. The wind and the sun played upon it, and the silent melody which arose was that dream-melody which belonged to these people alone, giving life and color to the self-absorbed and motionless hours of their existence.

When the guest had been bid welcome, and the first thoughts had been exchanged concerning the pilgrimage and little Sanni's death, and Palaga had gone inside in order to put her little boy in his cradle and to tend to her dead child, and when the children after a long period of intense staring had temporarily got their fill of the stranger, returning with a certain hesitation to whatever it was they had been doing, although still without having decided whether the new arrival was to be regarded as an asset or not—then it became surprisingly quiet out there on the hillside, quiet in a way that Abel Myyriäinen had never known before. The children's voices and their shrill little shrieks fluttered around him like butterflies, and the echoing evening heaven gently reproduced the various sounds from the pastures and the village—laughter and yodeling calls to summon the cattle, the clear tinkling of the cowbells, a fragment of a song a girl was singing—and the stillness took all these sounds unto itself, enclosing them within its mighty peace.

Myyriäinen thought of his mother for a moment. He saw her as he had so often seen her when he had entered unnoticed in the evenings, sitting beside the window in such a way that the light fell upon her withered face and her coarse gray hair, with her tired hands in her lap and her eyes filled with a melancholy which seemed to stretch its invisible hands backward to her own childhood, her own origin, her own mother. He had no sensation of pain or loss, only the deep peace of a perfect sense of belonging. Sinking down onto the ground where he stood, he spread out his arms, as if he would embrace his mother's lap; he remained lying there, his face pressed into the grass and his body utterly given up to the soft and shielding forces of the earth.

There Myyriäinen fell asleep as easily as though the grass and the trees and the heavy clouds had rocked him in a cradle made for the children of the giants. The tinker's offspring came up and looked at him and poked him with sticks and straws and stuck their fingers into his ears, but the only result was that he stirred slightly in his slumber. "He's asleep," the excited children cried out to one another, and it seemed to be a marvelous and incomprehensible discovery. Gradually they were called into the house, one after the other. The cottage door was closed, the people went to their rest. Out in the summer evening, Myyriäinen slept alone. The odor of the lilacs lay heavy and sweet in the sultry air, and in the dense thicket behind the sauna the little gray nightingale sat singing its elaborate and impassioned hymn to the brightness of the night. Thunder rumbled somewhere in the distance, some heavy raindrops fell. Violent gusts of wind arose, the trees bent down with a whining sound that was followed by a muffled roar. It grew dark, the thunder crashed like metal. The sheets of lightning crossed through one another, sketching quick and awful signs of flame upon the heavens. The passionate little bird fell silent, the leaves trembled, the whole of nature concealed itself and waited. Myyriäinen slept like a child in the whistling, booming giant's cradle of the storm, while the thunderbolts flashed above his head and the rain streamed down upon him.

Seven: The Lonely Child

Some minutes later, when the thunderstorm passed over the village where the church is, a fourteen-year-old girl, precocious and with a mind of her own, was standing all by herself in the park of the estate at Lintula. She stood quite still among the trees, her raven-black pigtails hanging down her back and her gray eyes shining cunningly below her bangs, while her soul thrilled with pleasure at the raging of the elements. She was still weak from the emotional uproar she had just gone through, and bitterness sat like a thorn within her heart; but in her spirit she was raised above her grief on the mighty wings of the storm. The sudden and threatening darkness which fell upon the park, the booming roar in the trees, the thunder, the torrents of rain, and finally the tempest itself enthralled her like the untamed and beautiful expressions of some primeval force, a discharge of stifled tensions, a purifying of creation's heart from all evil. Somewhere in the depths of her own unhappy heart the thunder's metallic tone found a reply, and in a dizzying second she experienced the indomitability of her own fragile being.

Sabine was not much more than a child, and she had led such an isolated existence within the closed world of her home that in certain respects she was undeveloped for her age; but she possessed a knowledge of suffering which could have befitted an apostle of Gautama Buddha. If the precocious child had possessed the great and wise teacher's ability to express the innermost feelings she had toward earthly existence, the outpourings of her heart would not have been so very different from the famous proclamation of Benares: "Birth is suffering, death is suffering, a common existence with a being one does not love is suffering, to be separated from the object of one's love is suffering, to lose what one desires is suffering."

Unaware of what she was doing, she arranged her life in accordance with a similar conception of the basic character of existence.

She was ruled by a secret panic, an insuperable fear of every and any change, and she took recourse to the most exquisite precautionary measures against it. She rejected every offer of friendship in order to be sure that she need never be exposed to the suffering which separation or spurned emotion could entail; in such case it was better to remain alone. She developed an admirable technique for sweeping away the traces left by the progress of suffering and death through that limited area of life which was hers. She cut herself off from everything, from gratitude, from obligations, from sympathy, from whatever it might be which could have involved her person in life's painful game of give and take, and she expended an infinite solicitude upon stylizing—and thus neutralizing—her surroundings, her own appearance, and her whole concentrated expression of the life within her. She sat before her mirror by the hour, lost in the age-old mysteries of the cosmetic art and, more than anything else, resembling a little priestess who performs occult rites in honor of an unknown god. The god was none other than immutability, the cold deity of the life-will turned negative, of nirvana. In order to achieve the appearance of changelessness, the strange child sat before the mirror and transformed her woeful face into a mask, a stylized image which forever remained the same and which she herself controlled: a sovereign denial of the weaknesses of her own nature.

From behind her mask she could observe people undisturbed, artfully deciphering the secrets of the world, without exposing herself to life's brutal caresses. She concealed her naked face. She carefully shielded her body from every contact. It was with obvious repugnance that she resigned herself to the necessity of having to shake hands now and then, and in these cases she offered a hand that was feelingless and stiff. When she got undressed, she bolted the door, and it would never have occurred to her to allow even her own mother to see her naked body or to have free access to the room where she slept. Her room did not resemble any other room. The walls were covered with the most remarkable and different kinds of things, shawls, draperies, books, heavy metal ornaments and chains; oriental idols and *objets d'art* shimmered in dragon-like evil and secrecy from all the corners of the room, weakly illuminated by hidden sources of light. Because of its profusion of contents, the room's effect could have been banal if it had not been tragic: a setting, thought out to the last detail, for a life which wished to disguise itself to the point of unrecognizability in order not to be caught by suffering and death.

There was something of a little Buddha about her whole appearance. She could sit for hours on the floor of her room, her legs crossed under her, apparently without having anything to do at all; the introspective, intense expression on her face bore witness to a secret activity of her soul which laid claim to all her powers. Actually, still meditation of this sort was the only activity of which she approved; she called it her "intensified laziness." Her absorption in music was merely another form of the same all-devouring meditation.

She sat before her old rosewood piano, stiff as a little idol, and played Bach, never anything but Bach. Since she had come to know the harmonies of the pious organist's world, sternly limited and yet divinely infinite, she would not have anything to do with any other music, to the great grief of her music teacher, old Miss Rosenholz, who revered Bach, to be sure, but who had given Beethoven her heart. She seldom left her room. If she did go out, then it was to the forests that she made her way, to the deep silence within the woods where some lonely bird let his trills be heard to the accompaniment of the harp-like soughing of the firs. She loved to listen to the melodic spirit of the water, not only down by the river but also out in the moorlands when the rain streamed down, or inside the house when it splashed against the windowpane. She had no one she could call her friend. Her only confidante was Lady Macbeth, an old thoroughbred mare which she sometimes rode. Everyone who saw the girl was struck by the oriental strain in her appearance and her manner. It was so striking that many, meeting her for the first time in the company of her loud-voiced, self-assured parents, asked themselves in their astonishment where the child had actually come from. But only a few guessed that her strange and uncommunicative passivity had its root in certain extraordinary spiritual experiences and in an abnormal sensitivity to the suffering which life contains by its very nature. Perhaps wise old Miss Rosenholz realized it, but she seldom came to Lintula nowadays, ever since she had got up in arms against Ottilia, the mistress of the house, on the child's account. The stern little face beneath the bangs cut in an Egyptian fashion became all the more reserved and stiff, the gray eyes beneath the eyebrows' pencilled arches grew all the more disdainful of the world.

It was not only the recent scene at the dinner table which

had driven Sabine out into the park this stormy evening. In truth it was something else which lay much farther back in time, in her childhood, when she was seven years old and experienced the major grief of her life. Or perhaps it was not this so much as all the other things she realized then, and which had turned her into one of those children who suffer because no one loves them. People generally think that such children are unusual and that it takes especially unfortunate circumstances to make a child suffer a lack of love in his own home. In actual fact there are so many children of this sort that the homes which do not have them are the exceptions; it is only people's disinclination to explore their own hearts and their inborn hostility which makes them unaware of the sufferings silently endured in a happy home.

Up to her seventh year Sabine was what one could call a happy child; she was not aware of her existence being different from that of others. She had her brother Joachim whom she loved passionately. The two lonely children in the big and gloomy house were entirely dependent upon one another's company. They were not allowed to associate with the children whose parents worked on the estate; instead, they meant everything to one another. Their games were completely their own and no one else's. The trolls in the forest and the river's fairy-like inhabitants who peeked up with their white faces when the moon was shining—these creatures populated their imagination and provided the material for strange masquerades, while the stories in Mortimer's old adventure books stimulated them to try bolder and more dramatic pageants with high-flown tirades and fierce retorts. The noble musketeers, Athos, Porthos, Aramis, and d'Artagnan, were figures they dearly loved, and even though the musketeers caused a little difficulty, because there were four of them and only two children, the performance of double roles gave a foretaste of true art's ambiguous fascination. They had their world to themselves, their language, filled with implications, and their secret understanding, and thus they had a part of their lives in which they themselves were the masters, and where they could take refuge when things with their parents grew too difficult and the home's latent tension exploded into frightening and incomprehensible scenes.

Tension lay upon the house like a brooding thundercloud and rendered existence unsure from one moment to the next. Although the parents were not aware of it, they allowed their own inherent hostility to reach the children through their manner, their tone of voice, and their impatient expressions. The children could not understand that Ottilia grew irritable and often shut herself up in the Blue Room for several days on end because she was disappointed and unsatisfied, and, like so many other women with nothing to do, abandoned herself to fruitless dreams about the Great Love she had never had the chance to experience. And they could not imagine that Mortimer, who was so big and strong and fine to look at with his dark hair and his flashing eyes, regarded his life as a failure because he was married to a woman who did not suit him and who poisoned his existence with her hysterical excitement and her false emotionalism. For the children, all this took the form of a dark and terrifying threat directed against *them*. The subdued hostility around them produced a feeling in them that they had come to this home, where no one loved them or took any joy in them, by mistake. They often put their wise little heads together and made plans to run away, one more fantastic and impracticable than the last. Their hearts throbbed with eagerness and their cheeks glowed, but it usually ended with their swearing eternal love to each other. It was in one another that they found a substitute for the security which they missed in the home, and in one another's love they found redress for their own injured self-esteem.

One morning the children awakened simultaneously and with a sense of anxiety. They curled up together in Sabine's bed and listened. To their excited imaginations the house seemed to be shaking to its very foundations. Uncontrolled shrieks alternated with hard banging sounds, and then it grew deathly still. The children were seized by an inexplicable terror. Taking each other by the hand, they sneaked out of their room in nothing but their nightshirts. Like silent little spirits they glided down the stairs to the ground floor, and then, their hearts in their mouths, ran through the deserted halls all the way to the wing that faced on the garden. When they had come to the little room which lay farthest away of all, and which for some reason was called the Storeroom and was not used for anything, they threw themselves into one another's arms and experienced their secret happiness in a rapture of joy. Solemn and wonder-struck, they touched one another's bodies and in some obscure way felt themselves to be fellow criminals and, at the same time, the only little children in the world who knew what it meant to love and to be loved.

The hasty caresses in the musty and almost empty chamber which should have been the innocent introduction to life's great wedding feast became instead, for Sabine, the harbinger of cruel death. Ottilia had gone away on a trip, and Mortimer was like a thundercloud for three days. On the fourth day Joachim fell violently ill, and not a week had passed before he lay dead. After closing the dead boy's eyes and laying him straight, the nurse had gone out for a few moments when Sabine crept into the room. Standing beside the bed as motionless as a statue, she gazed at Joachim. It was then that her face became frozen. She grew stiff in all her body, as though paralyzed. When the governess came rushing in and tried to take her away, she was cold as ice and did not move. They were forced to carry her out as if she herself had died.

Ottilia did not come home until the following day, after having received her husband's telegram. She found her handsome Joachim dead and Sabine in a half unconscious condition in her bed. Mortimer had locked himself into his room.

For a moment, Ottilia was permeated by the realization that everything she yearned for, restlessly searching for it beyond the horizon of her home, was to be found here, in utmost proximity to her, in the little heart which had been forced to suffer so. A hot and painful feeling of devotion to the lonely child flamed up within her, and a quick and vital instinct told her how Sabine must feel. She longed to be able to enclose her within her arms, smothering her in caresses and childishly tender words. But Sabine was as stiff and cold as death itself. Wounded, Ottilia withdrew. Things grew no better when Sabine recovered and could be up and around as usual; she rejected all her mother's approaches with a peculiar and wily expression which hurt Ottilia deeply. "Joachim would never have done anything like that," Ottilia thought, and thus she had returned to her old magic circle. She plunged herself into mourning for Joachim with that hysterical passion which she always manifested when something had been irretrievably lost. A phantom, and not reality, could open the deepest springs of her being. While Joachim was alive, she had little to do with him, paying almost no attention to him at all, but now that he was dead, she adored him as some higher sort of being, an ideal child whose like had never existed before, a little Jesus with bright curls. This adoration came to be pointed like a murderous dagger toward Sabine, who had the misfortune of being an ordinary living child. In her, Ottilia saw a constant, painful reminder of what she had lost in Joachim. Sabine was by no means as good-looking as Joachim and did not possess his special charm. In every facet of her being she was a negation of what had been so lovable in Joachim. Finally it became impossible for Ottilia to see anything but faults in Sabine, and she did not let a day pass by without calling attention to these shortcomings.

This did not mean that she loved Sabine the less because she mourned the loss of Joachim; on the contrary, her loss made her painfully dependent upon her love for her daughter. But the imaginary world in which she lived was such that nothing became real for her save what she experienced as pain and loss. Therefore Joachim grew much more alive in her eyes than Sabine was, and only those qualities of Sabine which distressed and hurt her—since thus she could focus her emotions upon them—assumed true life for her. With a curious masochistic passion she unearthed all the things about Sabine which were unlike Joachim and which for some reason or another irritated her, failing to answer to her expectations. She made no effort to conceal her aversion, for she, of course, knew that it was love which inspired it, love for the Sabine to whom she had given a transcendental affection and whom she had lost forever, love for the Sabine who had never existed.

Thus she shut herself up inside her own imaginary world, never becoming fully aware of the tragedy which was played out before her very eyes. Sometimes she caught a glimpse of the tragedy's effect in the dark flush which arose in Sabine's cheeks and in the quick and flaming glance which was the child's only reply to a withering remark. Then she felt unhappy and sat down in the Blue Room to have a good cry. But when she took out her altar cloths (she made a hobby of embroidering them) and lost herself in contemplation of the beauty of their sublime motifs, grief disappeared like a cloud from her well-preserved face, which was doll-like in its smoothness, and she could continue her embroidery untroubled, or abandon herself to one of the occult novels she always kept at hand.

But it was not equally easy for Sabine to escape the strain which lay upon her and which seemed intended to undermine her faith in her own personality's right to exist. Everything which wounded her and injured her self-assurance gnawed its way into her, forming a dark deposit in her soul, a dull pain from which she could never free herself. She could not even cry, for she had no one in whom she could confide. She did not trust anyone. Her parents' sudden changes of mood and their hidden rivalry with respect to her only strengthened her in her opinion that life was treacherous and filled with evil. She felt herself surrounded by hostile forces which pursued some end quite foreign to her own well-being, and which, whenever they wanted, could concentrate upon the task of breaking her will. Her manner, even her way of walking, acquired a crouching and creeping air, as if she were forever ready to take to flight or to protect herself in some other fashion against aggression. She learned cunning and craft, and her nature grew hard around the implacable determination to hold her ground and protect her own interests at any price, even though it should be at the cost of her own heart.

She often thought of death. When she awakened in terror during the dark nights of winter, uttering a little cry, it could happen that she experienced such an intense feeling of abandonment that she curled up in a ball beneath the covers, pressing herself as closely as possible to their soft warmth and thinking of death. It was such a consolation to think of death then. And whenever she was downcast, angry at Ottilia and the whole world, it was a comfort to think of death then, too. The death she thought of was not at all the same as the death which terrified her in reality, the death which came creeping up with its load of awful sufferings, the death which took men when they did not want to go. The death she thought of was her own trustful death, the last and most secret expression of her will. It was a great relief to know that such a possibility existed, no matter what else happened. A person could leave everything and simply die. Then there was no need to worry about anything. "They" could do nothing about it. The thought was a wonderfully happy one. It contained a seductive pleasure, a mixture of the sweetness of revenge and the delectableness of power, which quite removed whatever bitterness might cling to it. From death, this dark being, there emerged that single thread of power and secret redress which was woven into a life of helplessness and defeat.

Muttering, the thunder withdrew, but Sabine remained in the streaming rain. Standing beneath one of the defiant and aristocratic silver firs, she did not get wet at all. She listened to the mysterious crackling and splashing which passed over the earth, and to the heavy sighs in the crowns of the trees. A faint shimmer of triumph played around her thin lips.

The trouble at the dinner table had not been too much for her to bear. She had emerged without a scratch from many scenes just like it. But a single remark had broken the camel's back, the one about Joachim. It went through Sabine's heart like a sword, and then the whole world grew black before her eyes.

Ottilia knew very well why Sabine had sat brooding in her room all day long, and why she had not come out to greet the guests. She herself had ruined the visit of the company for Sabine by praising the good-natured girl's virtues at Sabine's expense, every chance she got: "What a charming girl, a real ray of sunshine!" She was all the more embittered because she realized what she had done, and was forced to take Sabine's behavior as a criticism of herself. Actually, there was something tragic in these violent reproaches of Ottilia's; and since, with her strange and all too mature perspicacity, Sabine understood a little about the way things hung together, she resigned herself to the unavoidable battle of words. The whole affair would no doubt have taken its usual course, with the exchange of accusations and the great outburst in the last act, if an evil spirit had not inspired Ottilia to say, as the worst reproach she could think of: "Joachim would never have done something like that!"

Sabine had often heard this very retort in her imagination; it had dangled over her head like an unspoken charge in all of her disputes with Ottilia. And yet it seemed as though life had fled from her in the instant it was spoken aloud. She stiffened and the food caught in her throat. She swallowed convulsively a couple of times, got up from the table pale as death, and disappeared like some mute and desperate spirit. Ottilia gazed after her, and her clear eyes held an expression composed of startled reproach and impotent regret, a regret of which she was almost unaware. She realized that a catastrophe had occurred; but she had not the slightest notion that she had touched on something which in a lonely child, even more than in others, is unbearably sensitive: its fragile and innermost awareness of being an individual, a unique being which has its justification in its self, removed from all comparison. Nothing can deal such a mortal wound to a child's self-awareness (which constantly has such cruel burdens to bear) as those criticisms based not upon the fact that the child is the way he is, but upon his being unlike others. Sabine's painful intimacy with the object of the comparison made the insult unbearable; her twin desires for self-assertion and self-destruction were joined together in a reaction which sent its impulses down to the very sources of her existence.

Sabine was just barely able to summon up the strength she needed to lock her door behind her. Her body was as if frozen, her eyes were dead, her soul had gone far away. She fell heavily onto her bed. Within her brain a single thought repeated itself obstinately: the thought of dying. Of not existing. Of being removed from the face of the earth. Of disappearing. She was not strong enough to decide how it would happen. She only knew that she would cease to exist. She felt neither rancor nor malice, only an infinite loneliness. She was terribly cold. Instinctively she fumbled for something to cover herself with, and when she found nothing she curled up into mankind's primal position, and was lost in worlds of darkness.

It seemed as though she heard a dear old friend grumbling somewhere close to her. She lay there for a while, listening to his growls. It was the thunder. She took a deep breath and stretched. Something untamed, deep within her oppressed spirit, could not resist the mighty explosions of the thunderstorm. When violent storms arose, she was seized by a wild happiness and could not make herself stay inside. It was her practice to rush outside bareheaded and without a coat, running and dancing like a foal among the trees. It was as though the thunder and the storm gave her a sense of those free and uncowed worlds where even the least and weakest of living creatures has its origin. She felt a desire to fly away in the train of the winds and, set free, to abandon herself to the turbulence within her.

When now, in the hour of her degradation, she heard the familiar sound of an approaching thunderstorm, a gleam was kindled in her eye, and she felt life come streaming back into her heart. Getting up, she went to the window. A strange and portentous illumination lay upon the park: a sharp yellow light fought in vain against the mighty darkness which welled up threateningly from among the trees, spreading itself in heavy shadows across the lawn and the bright red geraniums. The birds flew restlessly back and forth, and the smallest of the flowers opened their eyes wide in terror. Sabine did not hesitate any longer. She slipped outdoors, as if enticed by unseen spirits, creeping along with that extreme caution which had become her practice. No one in the whole house noticed that she had disappeared from her room.

She stood unmoving beneath the fir and listened to the stormy music around and within her. After some majestic crashes the thunder seemed to withdraw, and the rain enveloped her in its melodic roar. She looked longingly at the wet grass which shone with such a clear green light in the dark. She wondered how it would feel to be grass, dwelling in the earth and caressed by the soft and streaming rain. She emerged onto the lawn, and waded like a thoughtful water bird in the soft wet grass. Suddenly and without warning the thunder crashed, hard and metallic, right above her head. Her eyes glittered. The bolts of lightning came, one close after the other, and the thunder kept up its unbroken rumbling and crashing. All of a sudden, before she had actually had time to think of what she did, she began to run down toward the beach. The sky was like a sea of fire, and its vaults rang. Sabine ran as silently and lightly as a spirit. The rain whipped her face and her black braids drooped like gloomily folded wings, but her breast was full to bursting with music and her face was her own face, childish and cheerful, from the days before the great sorrow had befallen her.

Hurrying past the stable, she saw up above the doors the beautiful white horses' heads that she had always loved and that now seemed to turn and cast reproachful glances after her. Where are you running to in such a hurry? Why are you leaving us? She felt a sting in her breast and stopped abruptly. Not until that moment was she aware that she intended to leave home and never come back, whatever might happen.

She stood quietly, her eyes lowered, and pondered. The fact that she was going to leave her home forever did not bother her. Instead, she thought of Lady Macbeth whom she was now about to desert—she would be so lonely here, without a single friend. The old mare, grown useless, had become a thorn in Mortimer's side, and Sabine suspected that he would take advantage of her disappearance to get rid of the condemned horse. He had let Lady Macbeth live only because of her impassioned intercession. From the start, she had chosen Lady Macbeth to be her closest friend, perhaps because she felt that the old thoroughbred, put out to pasture, suffered from the same sense of loneliness as she did. With her lineage tracing back to the "days of the count," Lady Macbeth gave a certain aura to the ruined estate; and the existence of a link, no matter how fragile, between the estate's prosaic present and its magnificent past appealed to Sabine's imagination.

She had loved Lintula so much because within its gloomy salons and musty old stables and coachhouses it sheltered so many restless spirits from days gone by. As soon as the cabriolet left the highway and began to roll with a gentle crunching over the gravel drives of the spacious tree-filled park, its passenger got the feeling that he had entered an enchanted world which lay lost in slumber—it merely awaited a sign from the great magician's hand in order to arise once more, continuing the interrupted festival. Walking alone on a moonlit evening past the summerhouse, green and pagoda-like, dripping with moisture beneath the great elm, you felt your heart throbbing, and in the empty window could catch a glimpse of a dazzling white arm which sadly waved farewell to the cavaliers of the last serenade. Everything one had ever heard about life on the Carelian estates in former days, when Russian courtiers and grand seigneurs ruled them and when these isolated marches warmed themselves in the sun of imperial Petersburg, arose before the dreamer's vision in the deep twilight between the trees, and the air was filled with wondrous phantoms and the chatter of merry voices. If one's ears were truly keen, they could hear the clatter of hoofs during mad rides in the moonlight, and a coach, pulled three in hand, rushing past in a storm of recklessness, of treacherous intoxication with life's joys.

Nevertheless, the most mysterious spot at Lintula was the so-called Old Coachhouse, where all the saddles were stored. What particularly attracted Sabine, making her eyes grow dark, were the old-fashioned ladies' saddles, with their odd shapes and faded colors and richly ornamented mountings and splendid tassels and the brocades which were much the worse for wear; vague dreams of marvelous and intoxicating festivals awoke within her, as if love had cautiously touched her slumbering being with the tip of its magic wand—had touched it in that silent old coachhouse where a pair of swallows fluttered restlessly around their nest and the spiders had woven their webs over the memories of the past.

In some way, all these romantic things which satisfied Sabine's sense of the unreal had collected around old Lady Macbeth's nobly formed head. As she stood there not knowing whether to go or stay, Sabine felt that she would leave the fairy castle of her childhood in the very moment that she parted from Lady Macbeth.

Her shoulders drooping, her eyes fixed on the ground, she

began to walk slowly in the direction of the stable, and as she walked over the stableyard in the streaming rain, she suddenly burst into tears. She wept as though her heart would break. Her frozen little face was contorted in an oddly pathetic way; it seemed that subterranean forces had been at work in order to break the petrified earth which covered them. Who had ever seen Sabine cry? Perhaps Lady Macbeth had, sometimes, but no one else. People had only seen how her glance avoided theirs, and the tight defiance of her mouth with its corners drawn downward.

Weeping convulsively, Sabine threw her arms around Lady Macbeth's neck and pressed herself tight up against the horse's velvety muzzle. How kind a horse can be! Lady Macbeth rubbed her head against Sabine, giving her gentle little nudges with her velvety nose now and then. If an onlooker watched very closely, he perhaps would have seen a few bright tears in the mare's soft dark eyes. She loved the child. Under other circumstances she did not leave her stable willingly, for her joints were stiff and she gladly fell into sluggish dreams as she stood at her crib, her eyes half closed and her lower lip hanging; but when Sabine came to take her out, she felt a thrill run through her old body, and she entered into a curious kind of nervous excitement. When the girl rode her, she exerted herself to the utmost in order to imitate, in gait and bearing, the style of her youth. People thought it was both painful and ludicrous to look at; Sabine was the only one who completely understood Lady Macbeth and loved her for her nervous behavior's sake.

The horse's friendly and almost tender sympathy calmed Sabine. She avidly drank in the stable's familiar and beautiful smells and all its deep serenity, which had so often given her consolation and comfort. In a caress, she passed her hand over Lady Macbeth's silky neck, and chatted with the horse in her usual intimate way. The cheerful shine came back into her eyes, and she felt that she was big and strong, the master of her fate. She quickly leaned her cheek against Lady Macbeth's head and whispered quite gently in the direction of the horse's large mild eye: "I can't do anything else, you see. You understand what I mean."

Unnoticed, a rowboat was shoved off from the landing place of Lintula estate; it disappeared into the veil of rain between the holms. The old pale-rose house with the white pillars had lost its treasure. Hereafter no one would creep out onto the upper balcony, there to lose herself in contemplation of the arm of the lake, which mirrored the sunset in the water between its inlets, filled with a rank growth of reeds and edged with the weeping birch. No one would fill her impassioned soul with the sight of the brooding rocks, with their dark rust color, and the gnarled pines in the crevices of the opposite bank. No one would catch the sound of the wild wood-doves' cooing beneath the high and lonely treetops.

The river had received the lonely child into its protecting arms.

Eight: It Is a Pleasure to Meet

It was no less a personage than Assendorff, sometime horsetrainer in the imperial stables at St. Petersburg, who found Sabine more dead than alive on the second morning after her disappearance.

"Hey!" he thundered with his harsh bass voice, so that an echo passed across the silent waters. "Is that you, you wretch?"

He sat high up on the steep Maiden's Cliff, the special site he had chosen where he, in majestic surroundings and unbothered by stupid peasants, could reflect upon his life and remember the splendid days of his youth in the city of the czar. His nets and his fine new fish-trap had already been inspected, although the sun had scarcely had time to rub the sleep out of its eyes. He had just sat down at this favorite place of his, the smooth slab on the cliff's outermost brink—where he liked to imagine that the lovesick maiden of the story had stood before she threw herself into the depths—and was leisurely filling his pipe, when he caught sight of a neatly painted green-bottomed boat which drifted splashing against the stones of the beach. He peered curiously at the boat and saw a miserable little person lying curled up on its bottom. He realized immediately who it was. He lived as a lodger in the house of the old woman named Olsbom, and the sharp-nosed old witch of course knew about everything that took place in the parish. She had hardly got inside the door yesterday evening, barely giving herself enough time to babble the prayer which is prescribed for disasters and onslaughts of the foe, before everything she had heard in Matvej Olkkonen's store came rattling out of her mouth like so many peas. Imagine, the elegant young lady from Lintula had run away! Now they were making a careful search for her throughout the whole parish, and Lintula's master and mistress were beside themselves with fright. Broiling his fish in the embers on the open fireplace, Assendorff pretended he was not a bit concerned about the woman's chatter, but actually he listened greedily to every word, rejoicing in the news that things had gone wrong for the rich and haughty. He had been a coachman at Lintula for several years during the count's time, and they had never had a coachman like him there since, Assendorff thought. Instead of showing him due respect, they threw him out in a rather ungentle way, just because he had happened to get drunk when the countess wanted to ride into the city. He certainly had a crow to pick with Lintula, no mistake about it.

No answer came from the boat. He sat gazing at the miserable sight for a while. "The little wretch is lying there in her shift and nothing more," he thought, touched against his will by the child's pitiful situation. "Two nights on the lake and not a speck of food in the boat—I don't think I'd like to try something like that myself. Not even a rag to cover herself with. No, womenfolk can't stand that kind of thing." Like most irascible and unaccommodating persons, he had a certain weakness for children and young people. He wrinkled his bushy eyebrows and yelled with the full force of his lungs: "Are you cold? Are you hungry? Do you want some brandy?"

There was nothing left for him to do but to stuff his pipe into his pocket unlit; he would have to climb down and see whether the little creature had given up the ghost.

When Sabine awoke from her sluggish and heavy doze, she saw a great red-bearded face close up to hers, and heard a mighty growling which filled her with a vast sense of security. She was not at all afraid. There was something about Assendorff which resembled a kindly old thunderbolt. She looked curiously at his tremendous red beard, his small squinting eyes, and his peculiar ragged tunic. She did not put up any opposition when, muttering and swearing to himself, he picked her up in his arms and resolutely transferred her to his own rickety boat. He gave the boat from Lintula an ill-tempered kick, spat three times, and said: "May the devil take you!" Then Sabine laughed. She thought it sounded funny.

Assendorff was pleased by the girl's laughter. She wasn't nervous by nature, that was good. He pushed his fish to one side and put the girl on the bottom of the boat.

"There's nobody at Lintula who knows about horses now," he declared as he lit his pipe. "It was different in my day. When Assendorff came into the stables in the morning, every little foal knew that Our Lord had arrived."

Sabine sat up in the boat straight as a stick. What was that he said? He was talking about the horses at Lintula. Lady Macbeth's beautiful head seemed to rise up over the edge of the boat. She looked at Sabine with her sad eyes.

"Then you must know Lady Macbeth," she blurted out in breathless eagerness. All her exhaustion had vanished in a flash. Her heart pounded in her breast.

"Ha, ha," Assendorff rumbled. "I just ask you: who knows Lady Macbeth if old Assendorff doesn't? Did I train her or didn't I? I held her in my arms when she was no bigger than a bundle. I bottle-fed her as if she were my own infant. I have counted the hairs on her head, that's God's own truth."

He riveted his eyes on Sabine in order really to show her that she was not talking to a liar.

His effort was superfluous. Sabine trusted in Assendorff as she would in God the Father. She melted like wax at the mere thought that this red-bearded being had held Lady Macbeth in his arms when she was no bigger than a little bundle.

"Do you think that Lady Macbeth can cry?" Sabine asked and looked him straight in the eye. Her small hands were tightly clenched.

"No," said Assendorff. "That's something people imagine. What horses do is sigh. They sigh so heavily that your ears turn cold, in case you've done something wrong. Such a fine mare as Lady Macbeth, for example, has sensitive feelings, you know. That's what I've always said—you have to be a lady's man to get along with a mare. That's why I had such success in St. Petersburg."

Assendorff slapped his knees and let go a mighty laugh in his rusty bass voice. He told one story after another, for the most part stories of horses and women and that splendid fellow Assendorff who went around in riding boots and wore a fine livery.

But little Sabine had gone to sleep. Before she fell into slumber, she heard Lady Macbeth sighing. She sighed more heavily than any human can, and somehow Sabine got the idea that Lady Macbeth had a nightcap on her head with small silk ribbons tied beneath her chin, and she had to laugh to herself because it looked so funny and Lady Macbeth was exactly like the nice old troll woman in the big yellow storybook, the troll woman whom she had often impersonated, to Joachim's delight. Stretching out happily in the dirty boat, she fell asleep.

The sun climbed higher and higher in the sky, and the dream world of the morning, filled with presentiment, disappeared with its unspoken secrets beyond the holms. Clouds from the abode of unrest and change came sailing past, breezes swept over the quiet straits, and away in the edge of the reeds the bright-colored didapper plunged soundlessly into the depths.

Side by side with his own noisy voice, Assendorff's keen old ear caught the light and rhythmic sound of approaching oars. Swift and silent as a water bird, he made his boat glide into the narrow channel east of the Maiden's Cliff, and then went full steam ahead. The devil take him if he let the girl fall into the enemy's hands!

He took an irrevocable decision to help the girl in her flight. A little cockroach like her could always be hidden in some cranny or other. He looked fiercely in every direction, muttering half aloud to some invisible and garrulous opponent: "If she doesn't want to, then she doesn't want to! And that's all there is to it!" He felt in very high spirits indeed. No matter how you look at it, it was a joy for a fellow with the soul of a highwayman to have the chance of tricking authority somehow. He rowed so hard his horny fists grew hot. The water rushed and sang at the bow. Sabine lay lost in deep slumber while the strange beaches and the strange farms on their gentle knolls amidst the fields glided past, and an ill-tempered horse-lover steered the boat of her life toward freedom's unfamiliar coast.

Assendorff was careful not to tie up at the public beach where old Olsbom was accustomed to moor her boat. If the old battle-axe got wind of the matter, then the news would be spread all over the parish by evening. He had figured out a clever plan. He would tie up somewhere near the burial ground which lay on a lonely point of land at the edge of the village. It would not be a long walk from there to Uncle Ungert's cottage. And in the cottage, he had thought, the girl would find sanctuary. Uncle Ungert lived all by himself, except for his cat, and nobody ever came to see him. He would hardly notice that a little girl had come into his house, and if he noticed it, then he would believe that she had always been there. After all, the poor old man was always lost somewhere in his thoughts.

Everything went just the way Assendorff had planned it. The girl was so tired that he had to carry her. The creature didn't weigh any more than a crow. She hadn't had any food, surely. Nobody was in sight. He cut across the burial ground and noticed that a fresh grave had been dug. "The Lampinen's child, Sanni, is going to be buried tomorrow," he thought. "The priest will come to the village. There will be a party, and the old battle-axe will be gone all day long."

But when he stepped into Uncle Ungert's cottage, a stranger was sitting by the window, and Uncle Ungert was not to be seen. The cat rubbed against the stranger's legs in a very friendly fashion, its tail straight up in the air and its evil yellow eyes half closed. Assendorff paid special attention to these facts because the cat disliked people and spent most of its time out in the fields; he himself had a certain respect for the damned animal. He said good morning and laid the girl on the old man's bed. There was nothing else he could do. Of course, he knew who it was who had forced his way in here. It could not be anyone other than the fellow whom Lampinen was said to have brought home with him. What kind of a rascal was he? And what devil had shown him the way to the cottage? It wasn't so far away from Lampinen's, of course, but just the same! What was he prying around here for? The more Assendorff thought of the matter, the more suspicious he decided the man was. Gradually he worked himself up into a rage. He drew his mighty frame up to full length, so that his hair touched the ceiling. He stared straight forward and kept swearing softly to himself the whole time. "It's a peculiar kind of people who won't leave others in peace," he muttered into his beard.

Troubled, Myyriäinen stood up.

"I'm sorry if I've disturbed you," he said. "What happened was that I met Uncle Ungert at the churchyard. And we had a few things to talk about. He's very much interested in art. He has some handsome old prints he wanted to show me. Look here, what do you think of them? They're Leonardos, every one."

He laughed in a faintly embarrassed way and handed Assendorff a portrait of the head of Christ, so that he could examine it:

"When you see things like this, you realize just how little you know about art yourself. And how little you know about how a person looks. But you're pleased just the same. Pleased because it exists."

Assendorff could not deny that the man was very agreeable. He was not a little flattered by the fact that such a direct appeal had been made to his understanding of art. Yes, apparently it showed on him that he was something of a cosmopolitan. He spat vigorously in the direction of the hearth, put the picture back on the table, and declared:

"It's not so bad. Although I've seen more beautiful icons, of course. With more colors and things like that."

"Yes," Myyriäinen said. "There are many beautiful old icons, too."

As he spoke, he noticed that the girl had crept up to the table where the soiled old pictures were lying. She stood there in breathless stillness, lost in contemplation of the wonderful head of Christ. The vital, beautiful loneliness of the face fascinated her. She could never have dreamt that a thing of such beauty existed in all the world.

"Is that the Savior?" she asked naively.

"Yes," Myyriäinen said, and bent down over her. "Actually, one ought to see the colors. It's a sketch in red crayon. Do you like the picture?"

Sabine did not answer. She quickly directed her dark eyes toward the stranger. A friendly blue glance met hers. With a child's perspicacity she saw everything that was contained in it, the shyness and the melancholy and the strange blue loneliness, and her heart suddenly began to throb. Her legs could hardly hold her up. In order to conceal her confusion, she began to poke through the pictures, pretending that she was studying them. But all her senses were concentrated upon capturing the subtlest vibrations from this strange, strong being who seemed to be related to her, and who filled her with a longing she had never known before.

He put his hand on her shoulder. She was happy. Listening to his deep and pleasant voice, she wished that he would never stop talking to her.

"You understand what is beautiful, I think," said Myyriäinen. "You're lucky to have such eyes."

When he said it, it really seemed to Sabine that she did have eyes which could tell how beautiful everything was. She felt a burning wish to be able to show him something beautiful she herself had discovered. She stared with an apparent intensity at old Leonardo's pictures, but all the while she was frantically searching her memory for something which could give him an idea of what beautiful things she could see. In her haste she could not remember anything save the Little Mermaid, which she had once painted with her favorite colors, in silvery bright gray and dark golden brown, in order to convince herself of how beautiful the mermaid really was, although she had been made so ugly in the illustrations to Andersen's fairy tales. But oh, she didn't have her little painting with her! Everything she possessed was back there in the gloomy house to which she would never return, and she realized that she must begin anew with her two empty hands in order to convince him that she had the kind of eyes he thought.

"Do you think that the Little Mermaid is pretty?" she asked hesitatingly.

"I have never seen the Little Mermaid," said Myyriäinen. "But perhaps we'll get to see her some evening down in the river, if we stay on the lookout."

Sabine shook her head energetically.

"She lives in the sea," she said. "People never see her. But I'll paint her for you, and then you'll see how beautiful she is."

"Is that right?" said Myyriäinen. "Then I'll make something beautiful for you, too."

He felt a shy and terribly cold little hand slip into his, and two dark eyes looked up to him with an expression of such boundless gratitude that he almost grew frightened. He thought that he must impress this fact upon his memory—that he had promised to make something beautiful for her; for if he happened to forget it, then he would have committed an unconscious crime against a passionate trust.

"Your hand is like ice," he said. "You aren't cold, are you?"

Sabine did not feel that she was cold. She felt warm and happy. Her cheeks were hot and her heart throbbed within her breast. But still, it seemed to her that her legs were giving way under her and the floor disappeared and the room began to dance around her.

Myyriäinen took her in his arms and put her down on

Uncle Ungert's hard wooden bed, where an old horse-blanket served as a mattress. He noticed that her clothes were damp, and when he touched her he realized that she had a fever.

Blowing and puffing, Uncle Ungert came in with a bucket of water. He had some coffee beans which he had been preserving for years in a tin can. Now, by heavens, he would make coffee, for now there would be a party in his cottage. He had met someone who possessed wisdom about life and understanding about art. For a moment it seemed to confuse him that a girl was lying on his bed. He put the bucket aside and went forward to look. Sabine had revived, and returned his glance curiously.

"Why yes, it's you," the old man said, and nodded.

Of course, one didn't know what he meant by what he said. Perhaps he thought that it was someone whom he had known a generation ago. At any rate, he seemed to accept it as a natural matter that a little being lay in his bed. He did not take the time to think it over, for now he was going to prepare the coffee, and that was a complicated procedure. You had to hunt up something to roast the beans on, and you had to make a fire, and one thing after another. No one else was allowed to mix into these sublime and mystic proceedings. The water had to be clean, the beans had to be clean, the fire had to be clean. When he offered his guest a beverage, no one save himself was allowed to touch anything needed for its preparation. In every one of its parts, it should come from him, and be mingled with his life-spirit.

Meanwhile, a complicated and low-voiced conversation was taking place between Myyriäinen and Assendorff on the question of what was to be done with the girl. Myyriäinen agreed with Assendorff that, for the time being, they ought to bide their time and let the girl do whatever she wanted to. "A child is a human being too," Assendorff said emphatically. The only thing which bothered Myyriäinen was that the girl, judging by appearances, was coming down with a cold. "That won't bother her," said Assendorff, waving the matter away with his hand. "She's tough." It was decided to borrow a nightshirt from Uncle Ungert and to get the girl to bed properly; Assendorff took upon himself the job of hunting up a little brandy for her, so that her breathing could be put in order. And everything should be kept as secret as death. The two men were as excited and eager as schoolboys who are planning some prank or other. The thought that they could be here, taking care of the fine-limbed little girl and getting food for her and having the responsibility for her well-being, appealed to them deeply; their protective instinct was awakened, and at the same time their need for a tender romanticism found satisfaction.

Hardly an hour had passed before Uncle Ungert's coffee was done and Assendorff's fish were broiled and Sabine, all dressed up in a tremendous nightshirt which was carefully patched and so threadbare that it resembled a spider-web, got a hearty gulp of brandy which burned like fire as it ran down her throat, giving her a sensation of buoyant lightness and strength. If poor Ottilia, who had always seen her squeamish daughter picking at her food, had been there to witness what quantities of fish, broiled in the embers, Sabine stuffed into herself, and how she lapped up the hot coffee with it, she wouldn't have believed her eyes. Assendorff gave Myyriäinen a meaningful nod. "Starved," he said in such a whisper that the room rumbled and the cat spat in its fright.

When everything was devoured down to the last crumb, and that devil of a cat had got his share, Assendorff took a ceremonious farewell of the girl. He had one thing and another to take care of in the village, he said. He saluted

Myyriäinen and made him swear a holy oath of silence one last time.

Uncle Ungert, who was shortsighted, leaned over some yellowed papers which he had taken out of his hiding place. His old fingers trembled. The secret dreams of a shining and adventurous youth arose from these sketches which he had carried with him through two continents, and which he had always thought he would burn before he himself disappeared from the earth. Nothing of his spiritual person should be allowed to stay behind, adding to the litter of the world's trash heaps; he intended to take everything with him into the great transformation. But he had never had the strength to destroy these papers, where the frail and half-obliterated orthography bound his most intimate thoughts and experiences to the material world. He had thought: someday someone will come along who understands me and who feels the way I do. Then I shall read him everything I have written. And afterwards I shall burn it up. In a remarkable way, such a man had come to him now. He had not exchanged many words with the contemplative stranger, whom he chanced to meet in the churchyard where they were digging somebody's grave, before he realized that the moment had come when he would free himself from the last links he had with life.

He knew now that he did not have much time left. But he looked forward to a series of days during which the stranger would sit here with him, while he—slowly and without the least sense of urgency, leaf by leaf—would impart to him what he himself had preserved as the most authentic expressions of his personality. Even if it would be only a matter of days, for him it would be eternity.

He thought he would begin with Leonardo da Vinci.

He had noted down some of the master's deepest words, and because they had meant so much to him in the searching days of his youth, he wanted to read them aloud as the only real and true introduction to what he himself had observed about the meaning of life. The old Florentine, because of his all-embracing desire for investigation and his faithful, conscientious attention to details, as well as by the fact that most of what he planned to do remained undone while the noblest of his deeds vanished like a vision—the old Florentine was for Uncle Ungert the essence of man's astounding genius.

He suddenly looked up from his papers, as if he remembered something.

"You, girl," and it was apparently Sabine to whom he spoke, "did you know that Leonardo trembled, yes, one must actually say trembled, when he was going to paint the head of Christ on his picture of the Last Supper? And yet he offered the duke his machines of war. That's the way he was. And he wanted to make a flying machine."

Sabine was quiet as a mouse. She did not want to let the smallest careless word disturb this wonderful thing which was happening to her. But, all the while, she was sending secret little messages to her friend who remained in the room, although she could not see him from where she lay in the bed.

Uncle Ungert read aloud in his weak, trembling voice:

"Where the flame cannot live, there no creature which breathes can live."

"The origin of all our knowledge lies in feeling. Where the most feeling is, there is the greatest suffering."

"The deeper knowledge is, the more intense is love."

"If you, oh man, when you contemplate the wondrous creations of nature in my sketches, regard the destruction of my work as a crime, consider then how much greater the crime must be when one robs a human being of his life. Consider too that the body's edifice, which seems such perfection to you, is naught in comparison to the soul which resides within this dwelling. For it, of whatsoever sort it may be, is something which at all events comes from God. Consider how unwillingly it departs the body, and that its lament and its sadness cannot be without cause. Thus do not prevent it from inhabiting the body which it has constructed, as long as it will, and do not destroy this life in your deceit and evil. Life is so fair that he who does not truly value it is unworthy of it."

Uncle Ungert was overcome by emotion and could not continue his reading. So many memories pressed in upon him, strangely filled with life. He looked out with his old eyes, in which the dusk was falling, across the floor of his cottage, and there a multitude of phantoms came toward him, with hands outstretched and words that had never been spoken on their lips. "Yes, yes," he mumbled to himself, "there is so much which never gets a chance to live." He remained sitting on his chair, altogether still. Was he sleeping with his eyes open, as they say old horses do, or was he preparing to cross the boundary into death unnoticed?

Myyriäinen went across the floor quietly, in order not to disturb the old man.

He sat down on the edge of the bed beside Sabine. Soon they were involved in a low-voiced conversation. They did not tell one another everything that passed through their minds. Myyriäinen, for example, thought that Uncle Ungert was going to die now, but did not mention it to Sabine. And Sabine thought passionately of the soul's sadness and lament when it must leave the body, but did not mention it to her friend. Instead she said that she was thinking of the Little Mermaid, who had such a boundless longing to become a human being for a single day and to acquire an immortal soul. Now she clearly understood, she said, why the Little Mermaid felt the way she did. If she—Sabine—had not been born a human being, then she would long for nothing so much as to become one.

"But do you know," she said in a mysterious whisper, "what can turn a mermaid into a human being?"

Myyriäinen said that he did not know.

Sabine sat up with shining eyes. She threw her arms around his neck and whispered into his ear: "If a son of man loves her."

"Oh," said Myyriäinen. "Now I know what your mermaid looks like. She resembles you."

They both thought this was very funny.

"Do you think I'm pretty?" she asked.

Myyriäinen was careful not to tell her what his opinion was, but in his mind he was surprised at seeing such beauty suddenly come into bloom upon her face.

The very next morning, when Myyriäinen awakened upon his bunk in Lampinen's sauna and sleepily squinted at the sun which shone in through the open door, he began to think about what sort of beautiful thing he was going to make for Sabine. He had a vague memory of having seen something very beautiful in his dreams, it seemed to be some object which he held in his hands and which Sabine was supposed to have, but he could not recall what it was, or even if he had really seen how it looked. "What can I make with my hands?" he thought sadly. "I can't make anything beautiful, I'm absolutely incapable of that, and I can't make anything amusing either."

Then he happened to remember that Sabine was going to paint the Little Mermaid for him, and he decided to go immediately to Matvej Olkkonen's store to see if the storekeeper could get him some paints, it would be nice to surprise Sabine with a paintbox while she was drinking her morning coffee. No doubt she had completely forgotten that paints were needed for a painting, too, and that even a mermaid could not be done with dream-paints, in case anyone else was meant to see her. He jumped briskly out of bed, full of eagerness and the desire to get something done. It was a completely new feeling for him to have such a helpless being to think of and to look after. And then there was Uncle Ungert, too. He had awakened from his quiet trance with a remarkable sense of strength and concentration, and padded about his cottage all day long, as snug and comfortable as he could be. But he did not go outdoors, and he put the papers to one side without wanting to pay them any further attention on that day. When evening began to fall, he lay down—without any preparations whatsoever—on an old sheepskin beside the stove, as if it were taken for granted that the girl would sleep in his bed. Myyriäinen thought with tenderness and warmth of the little house which lay hidden and forgotten out there on the knoll in the forest, beyond the peaceful and beautiful cemetery, whose unpretentious chapel could have been taken for some plain barn or other, if the Greek cross had not gleamed from its grayed bark roof. There, it seemed to him, he had a little family of his own.

But when he stepped outside, on his way down to the beach to wash himself, and beheld the peculiar stillness of the farmhouse, which had been decorated with spruce greens, and noticed that everything was lost in its own special serenity, as if there were no people here who would go to the well or the pigsty, no children to poke in the sand and run through the grass with their bare feet—then he remembered that it was Sunday and that little Sanni was to be buried on this day. For a moment the image of her face hovered before him, as he had seen it in its perfect beauty that moment when she died, and then he realized that it was this face, carved by him in some noble wood, which he held in his hand last night and which he would give to Sabine as the most beautiful thing he knew of. He felt a mighty joy stirring within him. He went excitedly back into the sauna and closed the door behind him, so that the twilight was broken only by a faint glimmer from the greenish murk of the windowpane, which was no bigger than a spread-out hand; then he crept into the darkest corner behind the stove in order to concentrate upon that idea which came welling up from within him, hammering at his chest and the delicate muscles of his heart, as if it wished, piercing through him, to find the way to his hands.

Meanwhile Sabine awoke in Uncle Ungert's little cottage, hale and hearty, and immediately looked around for her friend. He was not there. The old uncle stood over by the stove, busying himself with something or other. The cat sat beside him and stared straight out into space with its round yellow eyes.

"Uncle," said Sabine.

She did not receive an answer. The cat took a leisurely stretch and padded across the floor to the door. Sabine jumped nimbly up and opened the door for the cat; sticking her nose out, she decided that the weather was delightful. "He'll be here soon," she thought, "and then we'll go out." She went resolutely up to the stove, where she intended to look after her small bits of clothing, which were spread out here, there, and everywhere in the pleasant warmth.

"Back to bed!" Uncle Ungert said brusquely. "I have some warm water here. You'll get it. And an egg into the bargain."

"I want to go outside," said Sabine.

"As far as what you want is concerned, I have your will in my trousers pocket," said Uncle Ungert.

"May I see how it looks, then?" said Sabine, and very gently lifted up the tail of his old frock coat. She could not restrain a little effervescent laugh.

"People are not allowed to laugh today," said Uncle

Ungert with great gentleness in his voice. "There's going to be a burial."

"Has it already started?" Sabine asked eagerly, as if they were discussing some special kind of spectacle.

"We'll be able to hear it from here when it begins," said Uncle Ungert. "We'll open the window and then we'll get to hear everything."

Sabine did not have to be told about it twice. She flew straight across the floor like the wind, the voluminous nightshirt fluttering around her legs. She opened the window as wide as she could and seated herself on the sill in order to enjoy the beautiful weather to the full. A big brown ant on the path below the window caught her attention. It looked so terribly comical. It crept with the uttermost care along a straw, and when it reached the end and could go no farther, it stopped, not knowing what to do, and one could see how unhappy it was. After thinking the matter over for a while—and unable to get hold of anything, no matter how much it waved its antennae in the air—it turned around and climbed back carefully along the way it had come. Sabine could not help laughing. Her eyes shone, and the corners of her mouth were full of unspoken wishes.

Then she heard the bell ringing, and grew quite serious and still. Ding, dong, sang the bell with heavy strokes. It sounded very beautiful and solemn in this morning hour. And suddenly the little bells joined in with an endless and jubilant ting-a-ling, ting-a-ling, which never stopped but simply kept on climbing and climbing in an infinite rhythm like one of the fugues of Father Bach. Sabine listened enchanted. "Now the soul is passing up to heaven," she thought, and it gladdened her that she had had the chance to hear it, for now she knew that the soul no longer mourned or lamented.

Amidst the sound of the bells, the little coffin was borne out of the chapel which stood on the birch-covered point; and, their heads bowed, the people walked beneath the bright trees. They walked among the forgotten graves with their grayed and crooked crosses which stuck up out of the earth like strange, odorless flowers from the fields of some other existence. Standing to one side, Myyriäinen, his blue eyes faintly veiled, gazed upon the gentle summer landscape: the wooded holms, the inlets covered with water lilies, the blooming meadows at the edge of the forest. In mysterious and joyful rhythms the words of the Byzantine ritual, heavy as death, rose up toward the sky, like an echo of the age-old lament of the human soul, wandering blighted in the wilderness:

What a mournful parting, oh brothers! What a lament! What weeping in this hour! Come, let us take farewell of her who but recently was among us, now she shall be lowered into the grave, the stone shall be rolled over her, she shall have her place in the darkness, she shall be buried among the dead, all her relatives and friends shall be parted from her now.

Wonder of wonders! What mystery is this which now has befallen us? How does it happen that we have been surrendered unto destruction? How have we been placed under a common yoke with death?

Woe, how the soul struggles, when it is parted from the flesh! Woe, how it weeps, and there is no one to take pity upon it. It sends its glance unto the angels, but it beseeches them in vain, it stretches out its hands toward humankind, but finds no one to help it.

For this reason, dear brothers, let us consider the shortness of our life and let us implore Christ to give peace to her who has departed, and to give great mercy to our souls.

The people stood in tight clusters, their faces pale, as if

they expected that the words' wild lament and the blessed joy of the irresistibly ascending melodies would bear them upward to the throne of the mystery, letting them behold the Resurrection:

Accompany, oh Savior, your handmaiden's soul to rest among the spirits of the pious departed and hide her in blessed life with You, Who love the children of men!

Little Sanni's face spread out like a fair and spacious countryside before Myyriäinen's gaze. He saw that trees grew upon its hills and the inlets with the water lilies were reflected in its peace and the fields and the blooming meadowlands had found their fitting place within its mighty contours. All that he loved in his heart's country was found within this face. It was little Sanni's face and yet it was not, but rather his face too and Lampinen's and that of the smallest child, and it was the face of the whole people. It was the face of man in the land of his heart. It would never die.

On this day Sabine waited in vain for her friend.

She had to console herself with Assendorff, who swore by all that was holy that he would bring Myran * back with him in the evening. Myran was the pet name she had thought up for Myyriäinen, and she had a great deal of fun imagining what he would say about it. Only many, many years later, when they both were old folks and sat nodding at one another, would she tell him how she had happened to call him that—he looked just like that big clumsy ant which crept out so carefully along the straw, and which could only return the way it had come. Besides, as the afternoon went on, Uncle Ungert began to tell stories, and then Sabine was lost to the world. Never in her life had she heard their like. She even forgot to miss her friend. If she had known that

* *Myran* means "the ant" in Swedish; the Finnish for "ant" is *muurahainen.—Translator's note.*

she was the last person to get to hear these tales, which had become a historical tradition in our village, from Uncle Ungert's own lips, then she would have been still prouder than she already was at the confidence which was shown her.

When Assendorff came to fetch Myyriäinen in the evening, the woodcarver stood outside of the sauna lost in contemplation of something which Assendorff—with the best will in the world—could only regard as a roughhewn block of wood, a block supposed to represent heaven knows what, perhaps the devil himself or his grandmother. Assendorff could not have been more astonished at the peculiar man's behavior: he walked around the block of wood in the oddest way, looking at it with a dreadfully strange gaze, first from one side and then from the other, and it was nothing much to look at in the first place. "This man is crazy," Assendorff thought. Myyriäinen did not answer when he was spoken to, either, but just stood there staring at the block with his hair on end. It was really uncanny. He looked so upset and his gaze was so queer that Assendorff contemplated the axe which lay on the ground nearby with a certain shyness. After all, he could not know that the man he had before him was in such a state of humbleness and pious astonishment that he could not have hurt a fly; liberated from that demon of loneliness which is the source of evil and of suffering, he was in harmony with the cosmos and felt a common bond with all things which have received a spark from the Creator's hand.

"Look here," said Myyriäinen when he caught sight of Assendorff. "I'm going to make something beautiful for Sabine."

Nine: The Face

They had discovered that, entering the thick green grove which lay right beside Uncle Ungert's cottage, they could be hidden there as if in a hall with green fairy-tale curtains which no one could reach and draw aside. It was a little piece of forgotten wilderness whose serenity had remained undisturbed since Uncle Ungert's matted old goat had gone to happier hunting grounds. The land was quite marshy here, and there were treacherous spots into which a small foot could easily sink. A mysterious bubbling and boiling could be heard in the earth round about, as if it were trying to say: I am the hidden river, the broad river which runs toward the sea. At these places the alder bushes, with their smooth bright stems and their impenetrable green arches of leaves, formed genuine little jungles through which they could walk, keeping a lookout in every direction among the ferns and the monstrous clinging plants, and feeling like the only people in the primeval forest.

But there was another place which the birds loved, and which Sabine called Noah's Ark because it was raised above the marshy ground and the invisible river; up there it was always dry and the sun shone and the bumblebees hummed like mad around some funny blue flowers which looked as if they had been made of rattling tissue paper and stuck stiffly onto long stalks. At the very top, on the shiny gray slab of stone which peeked out like an eye from deep within the earth, amidst stealthily advancing lichen and moss in brown and bright yellow and dark green shades, Sabine was accustomed to sit with her legs crossed underneath her, watching the exciting and changeful life around her, while Myran lay stretched out beneath the gnarled old ash tree which he loved, looking up into its many-branched crown and listening to the trills of the birds.

Nowhere in the world had Sabine felt as safe as here in Noah's Ark.

The epilobium, the wildwood's violet fire, stood like a row of sentries around her hiding place, the bumblebees' favorites nodded cunningly with their blue heads, and the yellow bedstraw spread its sweet odor through the still and sun-filled air.

Myran taught her to love the birds. One pedantic little willow warbler in particular became her friend. No doubt it had its nest somewhere nearby, and Myran wanted to show it to her, but no matter how hard they looked, they could not find it. Sabine could think of nothing except that nest. She crept around with all the caution she could muster, scarcely daring to put her foot on the ground for fear that she might happen to tramp on some downy little creatures in a nest. She could never have imagined that something of that sort could lie hidden between the bunches of grass. Now and then she heard an anxious and piercing wheet-wheet, and then she realized that danger was abroad—that she must have come close to the nest. She stood there on one leg, her heart pounding, and looked with all her might, but since her eyes were not used to the wilderness, she could not discover something as carefully hidden as a willow warbler's nest. She had to be satisfied with observing the little grayish-brown bird itself, which first sat in a tree, then hopped from branch to branch, holding an investigation in its own amusing and careful way as to whether there were any insects in the bark.

Of a sudden, a breathless Myran came up to her very quietly, taking her meaningfully by the hand. He led her cautiously through a raspberry patch and all the way up to the old gray fence, which was falling to pieces. At first Sabine could not see anything at all. She only felt the blood throbbing in Myran's warm hand. Going still a little closer, she bent forward, and not until she was so close that she could touch the fence was she able to distinguish the nest among the gray and stubbly rails. It was built out of sticks and straw on the most fragile of fragile things: a dried piece of bark already come halfway loose from the old fence post, and it seemed only to be waiting for a puff of wind to blow it down. Here the tranquil gray warbler had built a nest for its young in a strange trustfulness toward that strong hand which is the defender of the defenseless, the shelterer of those without shelter. Sabine sat down on the ground in mute reverence. The baby birds were quite naked, with only a few promising spots of down here and there, and they lay clustered together like a single, tender, breathing softness. She could see how the thin membrane rose and fell in the light rhythm of respiration, and perhaps it was this which moved her most of all, as if she had accidentally come upon something which was supposed to be hidden in the deepest recesses of God's heart.

"You have to be careful not to touch it," Myran said. "Birds are very sensitive. It can happen that they'll abandon their nest if a human being touches it."

Sabine merely nodded. She would never have dreamed of touching it. And she knew that, having seen it, she would be careful of everything that breathed—she would know that nothing was as sensitive and delicate as a living being.

Finally the bird itself came to the realization that whoever it was that sat in the grass close beside the nest was not some strange being, but rather something which had planted itself in the nest's surroundings, something that belonged to the surroundings like the stone and the bushes—this was how still Sabine sat in her contemplation. The shy bird seated itself on the fence post and sounded its quiet and modest cry: tsit, tsit, tsit. It sat there, quite content, and looked around; a frizzle of down surrounded its small legs; now and then it lifted its wings, which drooped a little, ever so slightly.

Afterwards, when Sabine came to sit down beside the big ash tree with Myran, she was so thoughtful and her eyes were so large and dark that he had to draw her close to him, letting her lie the way she wanted to, with her head tucked underneath his arm, curled up like a baby bird in its nest.

Myyriäinen lay there thinking of the wondrous thing which had befallen him since he had started to carve little Sanni's head. It seemed to him that everything he saw had changed since he had begun his work. The whole village seemed to have been transformed. The people looked quite different. Lampinen's face had acquired a certain remarkable quality he had not seen there before. Palaga's eyes had become as deep as the Madonna's, and her hair had a sheen as though it were in an old painting. The children had grown so full of expression that he thought it would take him years to decipher what it was each one of them had concealed in his dirty little face. For example, Mikko, who was ill and could not move, had shadows beneath his eyes and a cast to his mouth and his temples which Myyriäinen had never seen anywhere before, and at which he believed everyone would be astounded, if only they had the chance to see it. Assendorff, too, had been changed in some way. His ill-tempered old face had got something splendid about it, causing him to resemble a red-bearded Moses on Mount Sinai. Not to mention Uncle Ungert, who obviously declined more and more each day that passed, growing smaller all the while; yet at the same time he grew as big and tall as an archangel. Myyriäinen could scarcely dare to begin to study him, the way he looked now; no one could know, of course, how much time he had left; and, as for himself, he had only his own brief span of life in which to ponder what he had seen—and how could that possibly be enough time?

And it was not just the people who had changed. The trees had also grown full with expression. Even the ground had acquired another appearance. The special way the little paths had of creeping along beside the groves and disappearing into the meadows had somehow become mysterious. It was plain that the village roads and the black edge of the forest and the banks of the river all possessed an intimate relationship to one another, their emanations converging around an invisible center which was the soul of our village. If its writing could only be read, then the reader would behold a mighty face emerging from concealment. Even the little nest which had recently aroused Myyriäinen's amazement, hanging onto its fragile piece of bark, had its given place in that face, although one could not really tell, as it lay there, what its connection was to everything else.

He thought that, if he were going to succeed in rendering Sanni's face the way it was in the moment of death, he would have to include everything the village's mighty face contained, not just the faces of Lampinen and Mikko but the trees, too, and the small paths and even the little nest which lay breathing in the chink of the fence. It might seem that the task was one a human being could not complete during his brief time on earth—a task, perhaps, which he simply did not have sufficient power to complete. Yet he felt no anxiety; instead he knew nothing but happiness.

"It's really a strange sort of thing you're going to get from me," he said to Sabine, who lay with her head hidden beneath his arm. "It's not just beautiful, there's a kind of magic in it too. When you have it, you can never be sad. And the best part of all is that you'll never be alone."

He did not get an answer, and he wondered if Sabine had gone to sleep. He lifted his head to see what had happened, but then he felt his arm being pinched, and the pinch was more or less meant to say: "Don't look at me, you stupid Myran!"

"It's a dead girl's face. And it is so beautiful that, when you've seen it, you'll notice that none of the faces you see around you is as strange or ugly as you sometimes think. You'll be able to tell that, deep within them, they resemble the dead girl's face, and that there's something in them which is just as beautiful as the dead girl's face, although it doesn't always show so clearly. And the best part of all is that you can see that your own face is just as beautiful, too. For it also resembles the dead girl's face. The remarkable thing is that people don't realize that they resemble one another and that what they possess in common is the most beautiful thing about them, their true beauty. That's why it is so good to have the dead girl's face with you, for then you're aware of it and cannot feel alone.

Now Sabine crept out of her hiding place. She had to get a good look at Myran's face in order to see if things were the way he said. She thought that his face was very beautiful. But she indignantly rejected the notion that his face was in any way supposed to resemble Assendorff's or Uncle Ungert's. There was not another face like Myran's in the whole world, and that was the reason it was so beautiful.

"You don't look a bit like anybody else, and I don't either," Sabine said with great decisiveness.

Myran laughed at her, but she did not get annoyed,

because she loved to hear him laugh. Sitting up, he took her on his lap.

"Let me tell you something, my little mermaid. You can't figure that secret out before you've seen everything there is to see in the dead girl's face. It doesn't resemble anyone in the whole wide world, and yet it resembles us all, so that if we reach the depths of any face whatsoever, we're simply returning to it—to the dead girl's face. That's the way we human beings are."

"I don't resemble everybody and I don't resemble just anybody," Sabine insisted. "I don't resemble anybody but myself. And neither do you."

"If you knew how ugly a person is when he only resembles himself, then you wouldn't talk that way. I know, because I made that sort of image of myself. And it was a distressing sight. It was the dead girl who taught me that a human being doesn't look that way."

"How does a human being look, then?" Sabine asked suspiciously.

"What can I say? A human being looks like someone who knows that he is lonely, but who by virtue of this very loneliness is able to experience his community with men and nature. Can you understand all this? Whenever you are most clearly aware of being Sabine and no one else, then you are most fully a human being, and whenever you feel that you are a human being, then, in turn, you are very much more than just the lonely Sabine. You have a soul which can enter into contact with other souls, not only the souls of men but of animals, too, and even of the well-spring and the tree and the flowers. In this way, loneliness cancels itself out, and you become a friend of every living thing."

"It sounds like a fairy tale," Sabine said, astonished and a little perplexed.

"It is a fairy tale. But I can't tell it correctly. Only death can do that."

"Then it's beautiful death, not cruel death, that tells the story."

"It's only that we human beings sometimes think death is cruel. But that's not true. We'd be terribly unhappy and lonely if we didn't have death to tell us the fairy tale of our life."

It was time to go. Uncle Ungert was probably seated at the table already, waiting for them.

Myran got up and took Sabine's hand in his. She tripped along pensively at his side as they descended the slope of Noah's Ark; from time to time she looked up at his face.

"No one can tell the kind of stories you do," she said, and she thought to herself that it would no doubt be a great deal easier to live if a friend like Myran was always at one's side.

"And the end of the fairy tale goes this way," said Myran. "If there hadn't been a little mermaid whom Myran held so dear that he wanted to make something beautiful for her, then he would not have thought himself able to do something with his poor hands, and the enchanted face would never have come into existence."

"Say that once again," Sabine begged. She thought it sounded so wonderful that it almost could not be true.

Myran said it once again, just the way he had said it the first time.

And then Sabine thought that, no matter what the world held in store for her, she would never be able to feel truly lonely and unhappy.

When Sabine awoke the next morning, it was strangely silent in the cottage. Not even the cat could be seen. And where had the old uncle gone? She decided to lie still for a while and wait. The nicest part of the whole morning was when Uncle came trudging up to the bed with a glass of tea and a piece of sugar and a roll on a little tray, painted blue with a rose in the middle. He was especially enchanted by the rose, and always placed the glass so that the rose was visible. Then he looked at her with his old eyes and said: "Uncle invites you to eat." She wouldn't miss it for anything in the world. It wasn't a real morning to wake up in, if you didn't get to hear Uncle saying his piece in his funny way. And while she drank her tea, Uncle would stand there and watch, the way he was accustomed to do, for that was what made it taste so good, and what made it so much fun when the hard roll slipped out of her fingers and the tea splashed around. "You don't know how to eat rolls," Uncle would say then. But just the same, the best part of all was what happened after the tea. Then they had their little talk. There was nobody who knew so much about Sabine as the old uncle did. Myran didn't know a tenth—he didn't know a hundredth of what Uncle knew. Sabine had told him everything during these chats of theirs when nobody but the cat was there to listen, and who knows if even the cat was paying any attention as he sat there half asleep, with the one eye closed and the other opened just a little crack. She had also told about Joachim, although she had thought she would never be able to talk with anyone about that. She herself was astonished that she could tell about it, and without feeling at all self-conscious. Uncle didn't say very much about it, but he understood everything. Afterwards, he said that Joachim had to be allowed to live, too, and that's why he did not want to leave Sabine or depart from the house at Lintula. Sabine had thought she would ask Uncle a little more about this matter. When she thought about it, she could very well believe that it was Joachim who had sat curled up within her breast, for she felt such a pressure there. But after she had come to Uncle Ungert's, the pressure had vanished, and now she wondered where Joachim had gone. Perhaps he had entered into someone else instead. Of course, he would leave an empty space behind. Actually, there were a great many things she still wanted to ask Uncle about. But where could he be right now? Why, the fire hadn't even been lit. She sat up and stared uncomprehendingly toward the cold stove—the fact that there wasn't a pan of water singing over the fire seemed to be a direct infraction of the laws of nature.

Then she noticed that Uncle lay quite still, stretched out on his sheepskin on the floor beside the stove. She crept out of bed and went over to him. He was not asleep; it was really very odd. When she bent down, he looked at her sweetly with his old eyes, which seemed just a little absent-minded, and said in a weak voice: "Uncle feels poorly today." When he closed his toothless mouth, she could get a good idea of how sunken it was. He smacked his lips a little, and his chin bobbed up and down by itself. "My dear uncle, how old you are," Sabine said, and threw her arms around him.

Then, with a bound, she was standing again. She would see to it that Uncle had tea in bed, and then he would no doubt feel fine once more. Some dry sticks lay on the shelf around the stove, but she could not find firewood anywhere. Sabine thought things over for a moment. It wasn't as simple as you'd imagine to fix a glass of tea. The water pail was empty, too. She got dressed as fast as she could, wrapped Uncle's blue-striped apron around her, and went out singing to herself, the pail on her arm. "Scat!" she hissed, when in her haste she had almost fallen over the cat which sat right in front of the door. It did not bother her at all that the cat spat angrily after her, for she had more important matters to think of. It was an exciting enterprise to haul water up out of the well. She looked down into the deep black shaft and shuddered involuntarily. At the bottom, the water glittered evilly. It would not have surprised her if a long clammy arm had reached out and grabbed her by the neck as she leaned over the well's edge. Using all the care she could muster, she stretched her arm downward with the pail, but she saw immediately that she was a long, long way from reaching the water. That was odd. Imagine that the old uncle had exposed himself to all these dangers and difficulties every morning without saying a word about it! She saw that a rotted old piece of rope was fastened to the edge of the well, and it dawned on her that she was supposed to tie the pail to the rope, and lower it in that way. Immeasurably proud of her discovery and forgetting all her caution, she merrily heaved the pail downward, and almost went sliding in along with it. She uttered a little shriek, and, in her terror, let go her grip. Afterwards, it was a real comfort to discover that the pail had not vanished after all. But how heavy it was! She pulled and tugged with all her might, bracing herself against the edge of the well, but the pail just got heavier and heavier. Ordinary water wasn't that heavy. There was someone holding the bucket down there, that much was sure. "Shame on you, you naughty troll," Sabine scolded, and then the pail came up like greased lightning. She poured out most of the water, and as she did, she examined it very carefully. It looked like ordinary water, no matter what had happened. Quite exhausted but satisfied with herself, she left the well with just a cupful or two of water splashing around in the bottom of the pail.

At last she had collected everything she needed, a little water and some pieces of firewood, and no one could believe how much trouble they caused her before she got them into the house. Now—would you believe it?—they lay just as quiet and innocent as you please. But she was the troll now. "I'll scald your fine skin," she said to the water. "I'll burn you up," she said to the piece of wood. And she rejoiced in her heart when she saw the red flame, crackling merrily, devour the white wood. The water seethed and whistled inside the saucepan, but could not get out.

"Now you're going to get some warm tea," she said to Uncle. She was red in the face from her own eagerness and the heat of the fire, and her eyes shone with joy at being the master of the objects she had collected.

She sat down on the floor beside Uncle and gave him, as carefully as she could, one sip after another of the good warm drink. She let some pieces of a roll lie in the glass until they had swollen up and grown quite soft, so that she could give Uncle a few of them with her teaspoon. There was a funny kind of smacking noise in his mouth, and he blinked his eyes like a doll.

"I'd so much have liked to have a few days more, since it's not finished yet," Uncle whispered between sips.

"I know that you'll get to finish reading everything," Sabine said.

"How do you know that?" Uncle asked.

"Just because I know it," said Sabine. She felt big and strong. She knew everything. Uncle was like a little child whom you had to instruct—you had to straighten him out.

"It's so peaceful if you can reach the end. Then there's nothing left over."

When Uncle talked this way, Sabine had to remember Joachim. She sat thinking for a while, and then she began to weep quietly to herself. She wept and still she was terribly happy. She did not need to ask anything, because she knew everything.

"Just look there," Sabine said suddenly. "You look a lot

healthier already. Your cheeks are as red as a Christmas goat's." *

What the troll child said was true. He really felt a great deal better. He sat up and looked around the cottage. He saw the striped rug which Natalia Ivanovna had given him many years ago, when the children had sung for him on his birthday. They stood in the dark winter morning with candles in their hands and sang one song after another for old Uncle Mandarin. He laughed silently to himself. "I'm a winter child," he thought. "My mother was young and strong when she gave birth to me. My life was strong and beautiful. I have never been afraid."

With a great sense of satisfaction, he pulled himself up on his shaky legs. He had done many foolish things in the course of his life and had made many mistakes. One morning he had gone off and left little Katja, and afterwards he had never thought of her. He had tasted hunger and thirst. He had hunted antelopes. He had seen blood flow. And he had been paid back for everything he had done wrong. "I've lived, I've lived," he muttered to himself. He knew that a joyous death awaited him after the completion of his day's labor.

He got carefully dressed in order to be ready when his friend arrived, so that this friend, together with him, might go through what was left of the fleeting flourishes his spiritual self had written upon the face of the earth.

Today Myran came a little later than usual. He had been working so well, he said, that he did not have the heart to stop. He told Sabine that only now—after his conversation with her up on Noah's Ark—had he found the right ap-

* The pagan billy goat, which has become a traditional figure in the Scandinavian Christmas celebration, is usually given a bright red color.—*Translator's note.*

proach. Everything had become clear within him, and he had achieved the work's final form. He also knew what his sculpture would be called. Its name would be Death. And when Sabine saw it, she would understand everything he had told her about the way a human being really should look.

Sabine pleaded and begged to be allowed to see the sculpture immediately. Why, she could sneak over to Lampinen's this evening in order to get a peek at it. Secretly, she thought that if it was as beautiful as Myran said it was, and bore the name of Death, then it must resemble Joachim, although Myran had never seen him. But she said nothing about it, because she did not want to make him feel unhappy in case it turned out that the sculpture did not resemble Joachim at all. Joachim had been so beautiful as he lay dead that there could be nothing more beautiful than he had been.

"It can't be permitted," said Myran. "What would you say if we were discovered?"

"Well, you can bring the sculpture here, can't you," Sabine insisted.

"You can't move something like that around," said Myran. "It's as delicate as a bird's nest. If we move it before it's finished, then I might have to abandon it."

Sabine understood this argument. But it only made her desire to see Death's sculpture grow all the stronger.

Uncle Ungert was already rattling his papers. He carefully wiped his glasses with his big brown handkerchief and got ready to read. He cast a glance over the lenses at his little band of listeners.

He had not had a chance to do any more than clear his throat when Assendorff came through the door quite unexpectedly, a curious and important expression on his face. He talked as though something dreadful had happened.

"Trouble is brewing," he said. The Lintula boat had been found, adrift and empty, over at Ängsvik, and now some devil had got the idea that the little creature had gone and drowned herself. They had begun to drag the river, it was said, but nobody believed that they would find the corpse, for nobody knew, of course, where the awful event had taken place, and besides, the current here was so swift that it would not willingly surrender whatever it had once pulled down into the depths.

Sabine almost choked with laughter. Could you imagine such a funny thing! Now they were looking for her on the lake's bottom, and thought that she lay there gurgling with blue cockles in her hair and red coral flowers snaking between her fingers. She could see the scene quite plainly. Small voiceless fish came swimming across her face now and then, pecking at her cheeks and peering curiously at her with their round eyes. And there she sat, big as life, in Uncle Ungert's cabin, and did not have the slightest idea of casting herself into the water so that they'd be able to find something.

Myran looked shrewdly at Sabine.

"The stupid people don't realize that a mermaid can't drown herself in the water," he said.

Slapping his knee, Assendorff let loose a peal of laughter. He thought it was a witty remark. It was actually a little mermaid he had picked up that morning down below the Maiden's Cliff.

They could not take their eyes off the happy, laughing girl. The river had given them this child. The water's spirit, mocking and magic, dwelt in her laughter, and there was the glitter of moon silver in her gray eyes. She was very dear to them.

"Now we'll certainly have to say that we're alive, won't we?" Assendorff said contemplatively. "For otherwise there'll be a funeral. And that's the worst thing I can think of."

Sabine laughed so hard that tears ran down her cheeks.

"Let me have a funeral, I'd like so much to have a funeral," she howled, hopping around and clapping her hands as though to conjure up a completely new and quite unfamiliar sort of masquerade. She was never so cheerful as when the possibility of such mysterious confusions between fantasy and reality arose.

The strange chatter bewildered Uncle Ungert.

"Whose funeral are you talking about," he asked with a trembling voice.

Then they all felt a little foolish and did not know what they ought to say. Suddenly becoming serious, Sabine sat down all by herself in the corner under the old portrait. When Uncle asked about the funeral, it sounded so terribly different. It was nothing at all to joke about. On the contrary, it was very sad. She sat there, looking from the one to the other with a helpless and questioning gaze, as if she had the feeling that she was about to wake up from a beautiful dream. She looked at Uncle, she looked at Assendorff, she looked at Myran. She had a strange squeezing sensation in her heart. "Do you all intend to abandon me now?" she asked with a lump in her throat.

Assendorff wriggled around on his chair.

"What silly talk," he thundered. "We'll be quiet for three days and not say a thing. And then we'll see."

"Three days," Sabine thought. "Three days are better than nothing. They're a long time."

Going over to the stove, Myran pretended he had something to do there.

"You know how it is, of course," he spoke toward the stove and did not turn around. "You know what I'm making for you, and what kind of magic it contains. Then how could we abandon you? After all, we have everything in common, and that's what is so wonderful. And then you'll make the Little Mermaid for me, the way you promised."

The glimmer came back into Sabine's eyes.

"I have such beautiful paints at home, just wait and see," she said eagerly.

"Of course I'll see your paints," Myran said. "I'll see everything you have at home."

Sabine scarcely dared to breathe. It was marvelous to think that Myran would come home to Lintula, and she would have a chance to show him everything she possessed, her favorite spots and the Old Coachhouse with its saddles and the summerhouse and Lady Macbeth and, best of all, her own room and all the things she loved and had never shown to anyone. And the thought brushed against her like a breath of wind—although she did not want to think of it—that she would open the door to the Storeroom just once, ever so slightly, and show him the empty chamber.

The cat came up with a very meaningful air, too, and sat down right in front of Sabine. She looked into its yellow eyes. Tongues of flame seemed to spurt up within them, and dreams arose inside her heart like sparks from a distant fire.

It was like the beginning of a new and still more enchanting tale.

The old house with its pale rose color and its white pillars emerged in a wholly new light. Everything that was dark and heavy lay concealed beneath its foundations, and the house itself rose upward, floating in the magic gleam of unforgettable memories. With his clumsy steps, Myran came tramping up the staircase to the second floor, and in a flush of happiness she received him into her childhood's fairy castle.